Jeremy Wrecker
Pirate of Land and Sea

Jay Palmer

All Books by Jay Palmer

The VIKINGS! Trilogy
    DeathQuest
    The Mourning Trail
    Quest for Valhalla

Jeremy Wrecker
Pirate of Land and Sea

Cover Artist: Brooke Gillette

Jay Palmer

DEDICATION

To a close and trusted friend of many years
and a real pirate:
Bob Morris
who makes me pay my taxes.

Jay Palmer

'Not mine alone be this tale, but of all who fear to reap what they sow.'

Jeremy Albert Wrecker, 1597

1

THE WAYLAY

"A ship!" cried several shrill voices from outside our house.

Wooden plates clattered as my sister, Margaret Blythe, always the keenest for a waylay, dropped her dishes on our butcher's block and ran for the door. Kicking back our chairs and benches, leaving the last of our midday meal uneaten, our whole family followed her outside.

"Quiet!" Cousin Sidney hissed at my eager, vivacious young cousins. "Inside the house. Gerome. Jeremy. Check it out!"

Gerome David and I dashed off down the thickly-wooded trail while our complaining littlest cousins were herded safely inside. We grinned as we ran; we'd already had two sand-fleas this summer, and a third would keep our stomachs full and our fireplaces roaring all winter. To the port cliff we dashed, staying low, hiding behind the thick dried brush that we'd piled there to camouflage our primary look-out. From atop the craggy port cliff, six fathoms above the crashing, splashing surf, we spied through our best brass telescopes out across the wide blue Atlantic, scanning the horizon. On the briny, wind-swept, foam-capped ocean, under a sapphire sky, floated three tall masts of billowed white sails over a crowded wooden deck.

"Is it a sand-flea?" I asked over the roar of the surf.

"They're not sand-fleas until they sail into Gibbet Bay," Gerome David scowled. "It's a flea-bag; just pray that they're not thinkers."

Thinkers would ruin our day. Our last flea-bag were thinkers; they anchored outside of Gibbet Bay and rowed in a small skiff to search for the Golden Twinkle, our imaginary treasure, and then departed as soon as their rowboat was secured. We'd had to hide and watch, impotently cursing behind our piled brush.

"A schooner," I said, looking through my spyglass, "inside the inlet, coming straight at us."

"Pretty loaded," Gerome David said. "About sixty on deck."

"We can take sixty."

"Three of eight gun ports and two long nines in the fore."

"French colors."

"Let's go."

I jumped up to run back first, but Gerome David pulled me behind him. I twisted to tear free of his grip, but Gerome David was two years older than I ... and much bigger.

"Dog!" I cursed.

"You're a dog's pisser!" Gerome David laughed and ran ahead.

"You're what a dog's pisser pisses!"

Brotherly insults failed as we saved our breath for running, reaching home only a pace apart.

"Flea-bag!" Gerome David shouted. "Schooner, regular crew."

"Stations!" Grandpa Barnaby barked, his deep, ragged voice urgent, but everyone had already run inside, Margaret Blythe in the lead. Margaret Blythe reached her swag first, then pushed to get out as the rest of us squeezed past her. My bag held four muskets, six pistols, and two swords, and my station was leeward on the starboard cliff. I pushed through the others and squeezed my way out of our door, almost knocked down by Great Aunt Pearl, Grandma's sister, as she pushed by to get to her swag. Outside, I sped along the worn path, bending low, keeping out of view. If this worked, then Gibbet Bay would again run red, and the countless ghosts that haunted our family's snare would have new companions. If the fleas spotted even one Wrecker hiding atop the cliffs surrounding Gibbet Bay, then our waylay, and our family business, would be ruined, and we'd be lucky to escape alive.

Instantly I set my swag down, dropped onto my chest, and peered through the dried branches over my sturdy, musketball-scored log. Their taut sheets loomed closer: these flea-bags could be sand-fleas. In my wake, Wrecker shapes moved stealthily behind the thick brush that we'd piled and lashed down all around the top of our cliffs.

Familiar muted sounds reassured me: Grandpa Barnaby, Kenneth Joel, and Father were uncovering and giving our big guns a last ram. Behind me, Elviena Joan's swag dropped with a clack of musket barrels, and Margaret Blythe squeezed into her station past its dry, crackling leaves, shielded behind two boulders, only ten feet from Elviena Joan. I couldn't see Gerome David on the far side of Gibbet Bay, but he was there, watching the flea-bag and readying his muskets. Both Margaret Blythe and Gerome David got more muskets than I, which I resented, but they were far better shots. I set out my muskets and pistols Bristol-fashion, in easy reach. Twenty minutes after the call to stations, every cannon's mouth had to be cleared, each fuse primed, aimed down at Gibbet Bay, and every Wrecker hidden and ready to waylay.

I checked my muskets and pistols; each was kept ready all year round, oiled, polished, powdered, freshlyflinted, and with a ball rammed tight. I set my powder horn and extra shot right next to me where they wouldn't get lost in the chaos. My swords I set aside; if I needed swords, then we were keel-hauled.

Half of the sails were furled by sailors scaling the tall masts as the schooner sailed closer to the narrow mouth of Gibbet Bay; definitely a sand-flea. If they were thinkers then they'd have lowered all of their sails and prepared to drop anchor outside of the mouth. My heart hammered: waylay-thrills filled every Wrecker heart. Our littlest children, now safely inside our house with Grandma Lydia, were doubtlessly dreaming of the day when they'd be out here with us, preparing to fight for our lives and our livelihood; waylays were the best days ever, or so I'd thought until I'd lost my twin brother.

Dim, distant voices blew up on the warm summer wind, shouts from the sand-flea: they'd sailed within hearing range. I ducked low, cautious of the dried branches around me; a single snap of a twig could warn our target. We didn't want them expecting an attack, and I didn't need to see: the big guns, or better, Hammer or Fist, would signal the start of the waylay, and then all Hell would break loose.

Nervous, impatient, I couldn't help peeking, and a wicked smile stretched my lips. Our flea-bag became a sand-flea, sailing slowly into Gibbet Bay as more of its sails were furled. I ducked low; the sailors working the high shrouds rode their masts just below our cliff-height.

Carefully I glanced down through the dry underbrush; the deep, choppy waters splashed forty feet below our cliff-top, its current swirling eternally clockwise, rising and falling with the tide. Gibbet Bay was a small circular cleft in a high ridge, just big enough for a man-'o-war to carefully turn around in. Gibbet Bay's only natural feature was the Silver Sprinkle, a thin, pretty waterfall in the very back of the cliff, but none of the sailors were admiring it. Long ago, Grandpa Jack had hung a dozen corpses of sailors, killed in some ancient waylay, by nooses all around the rocky, wind-blown walls of Gibbet Bay; it gave the sand-fleas something to look at and think about rather than scrutinizing our cliff-tops and possibly seeing us. But those that could were looking past the Silver Sprinkle, through the thin, falling water, at the Cave of Riches.

The Cave of Riches was our great temptation, the secret of our family's success. No real treasure had ever been buried inside it. Zachary William Wrecker, Grandpa Jack's grandfather, had forged our first treasure map to lure the Weathered Dolphin, a schooner whose captain had keel-hauled Great-grandpa Zachary, into Gibbet Bay. Zachary only had Hammer, but it split the Weathered Dolphin's keel, and he and his two brothers ambushed and slaughtered half of the crew before they had to flee, and when they came back, the surviving crew had long departed. The ruined Weathered Dolphin and all its valuable cargo lay sunk on the bottom of Gibbet Bay.

"Weigh anchor!"

The strange-voiced cry broke the expectant silence, marred only by the peaceful, squawking gulls. Water splashed loudly; the sand-flea had dropped anchor in the center of Gibbet Bay, the current turning the schooner clockwise, its pilot straining to keep its hull from Gibbet Bay's rough, rocky walls, which would score their vessel like teeth in an apple. Their aft swung around into the lee of the port cliff; I grinned widely and gripped my musket, eager to start the waylay.

The loud *'chock'* of Father's huge mallet startled the sailors; many looked up at the brush-hidden cliff-tops for the first time. The crash of Hammer falling onto its oak supports alarmed them, followed by the grinding crunch of an enormous weight rolling down a long wooden ramp, and suddenly Hammer burst through the thin brush, flying out over Gibbet Bay. A section of a colossal stone pillar from the ancient Roman ruins that once topped this cliff, Hammer was a perfectly round column of white marble, three feet thick and four feet long, a thousand pounds of massive stone hurtling out from the cliff-top into midair. Instantly Hammer plummeted.

Sailors screamed. Hammer didn't strike center; Hammer collided just inside the aft starboard rail and punched through its splintered deck with a thunderous crash that shivered their whole ship. Seawater splashed up through its shattered core and the suddenly-yawning hole, showering its deck. Then the first gun blasted, followed by three more in quick succession. Thirty-seven cannons, each scavenged after successful waylays, ringed the top of our cliff, all hidden by brush and aimed down at Gibbet Bay. Father, Grandpa Jack, and Cousin Sidney were running along the ridge with torches, quickly aiming and firing each cannon. Timbers blasted into the air as sailors cried out or shrieked in pain. Many jumped overboard. Musket-fire mixed with the big guns, and Margaret Blythe screamed a screeching war-cry. Voices, Wreckers and victims, shouted through the sudden clouds of smoke drowned by explosions of gunpowder.

I aimed my first musket at a sailor running across the deck, fired, and watched him topple; my heart warmed at my success. Instantly I reached for another musket. Grim delight filled me; killing a flea per shot was the greatest Wrecker boast, and I'd been trained to shoot since I could lift a musket. I spotted muzzle-fire through the smoke; some sailors were shooting up at us: shooters were our first targets.

Everyone on deck was running, their muskets blazing, but we were shielded behind boulders and tree trunks, while all of their sailors lay exposed on deck. I blasted with all four of my muskets, and then grabbed my pistols, but clouds of black smoke filled Gibbet Bay. I couldn't target through smoke, so I hesitated. Gerome David and I guarded our flanks, Gibbet Bay's mouth back out to the sea, and our job was to make sure that no warners, sailors trying to escape by swimming, made it out of Gibbet Bay. I leaned forward to make sure that no warners were escaping, but jumped back as a musketball sang past my left ear. I fired both pistols into the smoke, then reloaded a musket, leaving my last four pistols unfired, ready for warners. I scanned the carnage for fleas and saw the great schooner already sinking fast: Hammer and thirty-seven cannonballs had holed it like pale cheese. Sailors splashed in the water like fish in a bucket, and our muskets fired ceaselessly all around the ridge.

"I got one!" Elviena Joan cried joyfully, incongruous with her shrill, thirteen-year-old laughter.

"Keep shooting!" Margaret Blythe shouted. "Kill them all!"

I hated my sister Margaret, who called herself Bloody Blythe. Murder by ambush was the Wrecker's family business, practiced for almost a century, but we didn't have to enjoy it. More than once we'd found a weeping sailor shot apart so badly that we'd thought them shark-bait. They always begged for medicines or asked for us to send a last letter to some distant loved one. I'd always felt sad for those helpless mariners, but I didn't dare voice my hesitation: it wasn't Wrecker. Margaret Blythe loved to shoot them dead even while they were praying. But my first duty was to my family; if word of our waylays ever got out, then the only ships that would come here would be the Royal Navy.

Gibbet Bay splashed, littered with bleeding bodies, broken timbers, and one fallen mast which a cannonball must've scored deeply enough to split. Their only unfurled sail hung shredded upon the foremast, brightly burning. At least twenty drenched sailors slogged up out of the water onto the lower stone stairs and fled into the Cave of Riches, darting inside for shelter. Gerome David fired a pistol and another sailor fell, but all of the dead man's fellows made it inside the dark cave. I rammed fresh powder and a new ball into my musket, pulled back my hammer and aimed, but by the time that my sights aligned, all of the fleas on the steps had vanished inside, though more were still foundering in the choppy waters; I aimed at one and fired. The sailor cried out, his scream cut off abruptly as he slipped beneath the surface.

I spied three bodies beneath the water swimming for the mouth of Gibbet Bay. Angry that I'd already spent two of my pistols, I grabbed two of my four remaining pistols and took careful aim. I fired one but the shot went wild, so I aimed the other more carefully and fired, but the sailor was too deep; he flinched underwater as my ball bounced off him, but he kept swimming. Finally he surfaced for a breath; Gerome David fired, and a stream of gore spurt from the would-be warner's head.

Another warner was slain by Gerome David before I grabbed my last two pistols and took aim. I waited until the last warner was almost out of Gibbet Bay, ignoring the musketball that ricocheted off the log by my elbow. Knowing that I was exposed, I leaned over until the last warner surfaced for air, and then I fired both pistols. Clouds of bitter smoke hid my target, but I heard his final scream.

"They're charging!" Margaret Blythe cried. "Aim for the Trap!"

I didn't have any rounds loaded, so I dropped my pistols and powdered my musket, rammed it packed, dropped in a musketball, and rammed it hard. By the time that I was loaded and aimed, fifteen sailors had charged out of the Cave of Riches and up the wide stone stairs only to reach the Trap, an exposed shelf, a wide ledge facing only sheer rock twenty feet below the top of the cliff. We used a long ladder to reach the Trap, but we always removed the ladder after each salvage. From the Trap, the only path upwards was a narrow ridge carved to look (from below) like stairs that went all the way to the top. We kids could scale that false stair to the ridge, moving slowly and carefully, but the soaked, sword-wielding sailors were trapped, each Wrecker firing at them as fast as we could reload. Some sailors tried to run back down to the safety of the Cave of Riches while others jumped off the ledge back into the water. I aimed at one running back down; those who jumped into the water would never make it back. They weren't even firing anymore; all of their powder was spent or soaked, so most of us Wreckers stood on our feet, firing at will.

At least two sailors dashed safely back into the Cave of Riches, one of whom was wounded, his bare back streaming blood. Corpses filled the water, floating just under the surface. There were more fleas than we'd

thought; at least eighty men had sailed into Gibbet Bay
on an armed schooner, but Hammer, thirty-seven
cannons, and fourteen of us, with sixty-three muskets
and eighty-eight pistols, and little Hunter Jack, who was
too young to shoot but liked to drop old cannonballs
onto swimming sailors, had easily sent them to Davey
Jones' locker. Our cannons had probably taken out
most of the fleas; our waylay had caught them
unprepared, and those who ran below decks to get their
muskets were probably sliced to ribbons as cannon-
shattered planks were blasted into flying shards, splinters
as big as your hand, or drowned when the schooner
sank. The rest of the sailors were mostly unarmed, easy
targets, with nowhere to go except to try and swim out of
the mouth of Gibbet Bay or climb the exposed steps to
the Cave of Riches, which was a deathtrap. The Golden
Twinkle existed only in the imaginations of those who
came looking for buried treasure; inside the Cave of
Riches lay only three large, empty chests, two skeletons,
a few half-buried copper coins, and a poisoned bottle of
rum, all arranged in a small pit to look like pirate
treasure had once been buried there but was long ago
ransacked. Grandma Agnes made the rum; she called it
her hangover-proof grog, spiced with cinnamon and
pepper, which hid the taste of the deadly belladonna
berries which Grandma Agnes had us collect and
squeeze every spring. It often ended the same when
sailors took refuge in the Cave of Riches; they'd find the

rum, pass it around, and fifteen minutes later they'd all be choking, turning green, and gasping their last breaths.

The cracks of our muskets ceased. We'd won again. Cousin Sidney and Kenneth Joel cheered, and soon all of us were shouting for joy. Two fishing ships had already been waylaid this year. Now we'd sunk a valuable schooner, and it was only the end of summer. I cheered along with the others, but the bloody carnage below suddenly turned my stomach in a most un-Wreckerly way. My twin brother, Chad Mathew Wrecker, had died only two months ago at our last waylay, shot through his young heart. Although I was glad to avenge him, no waylay would bring him back; I was the first Wrecker to stop cheering.

"Parley!"

The desperate cry echoed up from the Cave of Riches, which was clearly visible behind the Silver Sprinkle. We all laughed. Olivia Frances fired a musketball into the cave; it kicked up dust and ricocheted against the inside wall, and Margaret Blythe fired a shot to match it, but Grandpa Barnaby shouted at both of them.

"Muskets down! Respect parley!"

Neither woman dropped their musket. Margaret Blythe lifted her powder horn with a grin and started to reload.

"You ... in the cave!" Grandpa Barnaby shouted. "What do you want?"

"To live, good master!" the voice pleaded. "Just let us go. We've no weapons, no money, just poor Christian souls not prepared for Heaven. Pray, let us go and we'll never return!"

"Lying's a violation of parley!" Grandpa Barnaby shouted angrily. "Christians? I doubt if any of you've seen the inside of a church for years. Say your prayers, if Christians you be. Prepare yourselves, for by the honor of parley, I speak only truth: none escape Gibbet Bay."

No reply came to this pronouncement of doom. In the silence, broken only by the gusty wind, a few chirping sparrows, and the sorrowful cries of distant gulls, I stared at Grandpa Barnaby admiringly; a true sea salt, Grandpa Barnaby had left the Wrecker clan for many years and gone to sea, wanting a ship of his own that we hadn't demolished into kindling. Eventually he'd returned, weary and disgusted, having never achieved his goal, a true corsair's Bosun, a man of the sea, but never a captain.

Grandpa Barnaby nodded to Cousin Sidney, who smiled and jumped to. The hangover-proof grog would eventually take them out, but that could take hours or days. We'd have no signal, so we would have to stand guard over the cave's entrance night and day, and then finally go down ourselves, muskets loaded, to make sure that all of the fleas were dead. Cousin Sidney had a better way.

Cousin Sidney took a small, recently-washed, sealed barrel of gunpowder which he'd thickly wrapped with

dry rags and bound with a long rope. He measured out
the rope exactly and tied its other end to a tree trunk at
the top of the cliff right beside the Silver Sprinkle, and
then he dug his fingers into a waiting bucket of oily
bacon grease and pig-fat. He smeared the slimy,
flammable mixture all over the dry rags. The rags
soaked up the oil, and when he set a flame to the rags,
they quickly blazed up. Finally, Cousin Sidney gave a
great laugh, lifted the flaming powder-barrel over his
head, took quick aim, and hurled it out over Gibbet Bay.

We ducked for cover. The fiery powder barrel fell,
sprung as its rope stretched taut, and swung all the way
down, right inside the Cave of Riches. It didn't explode
at once, as it sometimes did, especially when Cousin
Sidney missed and it smashed against the rocks outside
the cave, blasting and blackening only bare stone. The
trapped sailors cried out and shouted fearfully, but none
dared approach the flaming barrel. Only seconds
passed; the wide wax seals containing the dangerous
gunpowder inside the barrel quickly melted in the
flames, exposing the explosive mixture. The ground
sulfur, coal, and saltpeter detonated in a fireball that
rocked the cliffs and deafened us, louder than any
cannon-fire. Cousin Sidney cheered and grabbed his
musket, aiming straight down at the cave mouth.
Possibly the exploded cask had finished off the sailors,
but soon the silence after the *bang!* was broken by loud
coughing. Thick black smoke poured from the Cave of
Riches, and suddenly a figure burst out, running for his

life. He dove through the Silver Sprinkle into the corpse-strewn, bloody waters of Gibbet Bay. Six shots fired as he dove, but none seemed to hit him; he splashed in, dove deep, and his passage was instantly hidden by the flotsam of his ruined ship and dead mates. But he couldn't stay underwater forever; the schooner's deck had sunk beneath the surface, and little concealment and no protection was offered by the two remaining masts still poking up out of the water.

Another sailor came staggering, choking and coughing, out of the Cave of Riches. He didn't make it past the landing; Elviena Joan and Grandma Agnes fired, and he collapsed onto the stone ledge into the splash of the Silver Sprinkle. Gerome David and several others fired their last rounds, and the barely-underwater would-be warner jerked and sank just past the floating topsails of the fallen mizzenmast. Then we all stood and looked down, watching for any movement not caused by the constant rocking of the sea.

"Deathwatch!" Grandpa Barnaby shouted, and most of the elders dropped their muskets to their sides. Our waylay was over. Several started gathering weapons and repacking their swags, but Gerome David and Bloody Blythe reloaded and stood watching down their sights, searching for any sign of life. I didn't set my musket down but turned to look out at the wide, endless sea, and wondered what other lives were out there, normal lives where people didn't kill other people, anywhere but here. This was my first waylay without my dear twin brother; the first waylay that didn't delight me.

An hour later, convinced that no survivors threatened us, Grandpa Jack sent me, Father, Gerome David, Margaret Blythe, and Hunter Jack to start the Sharking. Our rowboat, which we lowered down the cliff with the small winch, slipped onto the water. We lowered our long ladder and descended to the Trap atop the upper-stairs, stripping the sailor's corpses of all valuables and then kicking them off into the water. Margaret Blythe found a small coin-purse on one man and Hunter Jack found a good musket, and we collected several copper rings, knives, and a fancy sword even before we made it to the Cave of Riches. Ignoring the dead, Father and Gerome David went straight down, a pistol in each hand; Olivia Frances and Kenneth Joel were still watching from above, several loaded muskets ready, but they couldn't shoot inside the Cave of Riches. Sticking a pistol into his belt, Father pulled out a silver mirror, which he slowly held out before the mouth of the cave, examining everything that he could see before exposing himself.

"Anyone alive?" Father called.

No one replied, but that didn't prove anything. Father pocketed the mirror and drew his second pistol. He nodded to Gerome David, and then both of them jumped in front of the cave-mouth, each firing one pistol into the darkness inside. One long moment they stared, frozen, ready, and then they entered the cave. I turned away, looking at all of the dead sailors floating in the water, scanning for anything that might be valuable. The schooner's sunken prow was visible below the bloody water: The Scarlet Siren, its letters read. No one would ever know what became of it; a noble ship, soon to be our winter firewood. It seemed a great waste; I wondered what it'd be like to stand aboard a fast-sailing ship that wasn't a sunken wreck.

Sharking is ugly; waylays attract sharks, so we have to haul away the dead as fast as possible. One by one we hooked and raised their corpses, and then pulled off their rings, necklaces, belts, vests, shoes, earrings; anything that we liked. Margaret Blythe sat in the back of the boat with two loaded pistols, eager to kill anything still alive. Hunter Jack, who was almost twelve, and Margaret Blythe kept pointing out exceptionally-nasty wounds, many of which Margaret boasted of having personally inflicted. Hunter Jack complained that he was big enough to shoot, but the recoil of every musket that we'd ever given him knocked him backwards, off his feet. After searching each body, we tied a hitch around one leg, and then we rowed into the surf outside the mouth of Gibbet Bay, trailing a line of twenty floating sailors on each trip. Gibbet Bay was part of a great inlet that led nowhere, so only ships seeking the Golden Twinkle ever came here. A mile outside of Gibbet Bay we untied the dead bodies, leaving the bloody rope in the water so that the rocking sea would scrub it clean, and we rowed back.

Elviena Joan sat in Gerome David's station at the top of the mouth, keeping watch for other flea-bags; rotten luck it would be to have a man-'o-war sail up while we sat adrift in a rowboat with a fish-line of corpses. We didn't expect any more visitors; only one Lure was sent out at a time. If news of our waylays ever got out, even if we escaped the vengeful sailors, we'd be lucky to survive. We'd have to flee into the hills, and months might pass before we could come back home, and we'd never get to waylay again.

Sharking helped conceal us; accustomed to feeding here, sharks frequented Gibbet Bay, and the local fishermen preferred safer waters. The sun was setting by the time that we released the last of our floating dead to the tide. Under darkening skies we rowed back, wary of sharks; Gibbet Bay would remain pink for days. There were undoubtedly corpses still trapped inside its sunken hull, but it was too late to start the Salvage, and they weren't going anywhere. We tied our rowboat before the Cave of Riches, then washed our many new prizes, and ourselves, in the cascading Silver Sprinkle. I washed longer than ever, but I still felt dirty.

Jay Palmer

2

THE BIBLE

"Bless you!" Great Aunt Pearl's screechy voice cackled with merriment.

"Jeremy Albert found the pearl ring," Father grinned.

Pearl hurried forward and hugged me tightly. I squirmed uncomfortably; my great-aunt squeezed me against her sagging, aged flesh, her round treasures clicking over her floppy breasts; pearls were her beloved favorites. Grandma Agnes' sister, Vivian Rose Wrecker insisted that everyone call her Pearl after her adored treasures, of which she wore eight rings and eleven strands. Pearl tolerated no one to keep a pearl unless she gave it to them. Her eyesight was poor; after the initial volley, Pearl just reloaded for others, but she was mistress of our kitchen and oversaw every meal. I grimaced as she held up her new pearl ring before my eyes.

"Jeremy Albert Wrecker!" Pearl almost sang my name. "A blue pearl; very rare! I'll cook something special for you!"

Mother scowled and held out a plate of thick cheese slices.

"Just one, Jeremy Albert, and some bread, and then to bed," Mother said. "Hurry; we've got to read."

Everyone frowned at this dreaded pronouncement; Mother read from the family bible after every waylay. I took a slice of cheese and tore off a large chunk of bread, then quickly ate both. With luck, I'd be asleep before Mother finished Great-grandpa Zachary's inscription.

Uncle Rory brought Mother Great-grandpa Zachary's bible and a candle to read it by. I stuffed the last of my bread into my mouth, then crawled into bed, making Hunter Jack, Kevin John, Devin Elliot, and Brad Eaton scoot over. I laid back and stared up at our thick wooden rafters. Our house was a small, one-room stone fortress. Once, a luxurious Roman villa with a tower overlooked our seascape, occupied by a garrison of Roman soldiers, until the Celtic tribes killed them and burned their villa. Few ruins remained; the Wrecker house was once a small hall that Great-grandpa Zachary and his brothers had rebuilt from the ruins and topped with a sturdy wooden roof, first built of timbers from the Weathered Dolphin's hull. A wide, round fire pit lay in the center of our house, under our copper-fitted chimney. Great Aunt Pearl's kitchen table stood on one side of our fire pit, and four strong tables with benches sat on the other side. Each wall had its own set of beds; the boys by the door, girls near the window, old folks opposite the girls, and parents in the back behind the kitchen. Dividing our beds were huge shelves packed with prizes from past waylays: muskets and pistols, musical instruments, fancy clocks, unbroken portals, statuary and telescopes, sextons and jeweled music boxes, silver hair combs and mirrors, and knives and cutlasses beyond count. Everything that we'd ever scavenged lay stacked in thick piles, and this was only the recent overflow; these cliffs were filled with tiny caves. Rumors told that Grandpa Jack, Grandpa Barnaby, and Kenneth Joel had filled more than one cave with valuable plunder, then sealed them up. We kids had searched our whole lives, our own youthful treasure hunt, but never found one. If the Wrecker clan was ever discovered and had to flee, eventually we'd come back and recover our buried wealth. We kids knew was that those sealed caves had to exist; if over a century of plunder had been stored in our house then it'd be piled from floor to roof.

Mother read the inscription on the inside cover of the bible written in Great-grandpa Zachary's wide, looping handwriting.

Blessed be God Almighty from whom all swags flow. His grace upon the Wrecker family and forgiveness for our sins, for which we give eternal thanks. No commandment shall we break, save to feed and spare our family, and to protect our children and loved ones.

To all my children, never forget these words: God favors each man independently. Some are blessed with great wealth, others with long life, and others with eternal happiness; the generosity of God must be met with equal determination to keep his gifts, for the greatest sin is to squander the bounty that He bestows. All that we own would be taken from us if the secret of the success which God bestowed upon us were ever revealed, so humbly protect His gift, Gibbet Bay, knowing that paradise everlasting awaits for those who support God's will.

With infinite devotion,
Zachary William Wrecker
Founder and Father
The Wrecker Clan

Mother then flipped through the thick bible to some random page and began reading, but I closed my eyes and her words blurred and faded away.

"Salvage!"

Gibbet Bay shined brightly in the morning light. Piled by the current, the tide-washed wreckage of broken timbers and flotsam bobbed on the choppy water under the lee of the starboard cliff. Two bodies floated amid the clutter; either they'd been flushed out of the ruined hull or floated back inside after the Sharking. It didn't matter; the water was mostly blue, the waves steady, and no fins showed.

"Ready the anchor," Grandpa Barnaby said.

Gerome David and I took a long, stout rope and headed in opposite directions. I jumped the Silver Sprinkle, listening to the stream's tinkling waters splash over the edge, down toward the Cave of Riches, while Gerome David headed for the opposite cliff. Walking carefully around our cliff-top, we strung our long, heavy rope clear across the wide gulf, from port cliff to starboard cliff, until it spanned Gibbet Bay. I tied my end of our rope securely around the big tree on the port cliff and then hurried back. Gerome David looped his end of the rope through the stone anchor's pulley and wound it tight onto the big winch.

Salvaged off a man-'o-war, with all of us working it, our big winch could haul up Hammer and Fist; compared to them, our anchor was light. Grandpa Barnaby, Father, and Gerome David heaved to; our anchor was a heavy stone block, two hundred pounds, with a wide, well-greased iron pulley sticking out of its top. Using the winch, Grandpa Barnaby, Father, and Gerome David lifted the anchor a few inches, and then Margaret Blythe and I shoved it over the edge until the great weight hung free over the bay.

"That's enough!" Father shouted. "Back slow!"

Carefully we reversed the winch, lowering the great,

heavy stone anchor which, its pulley taut upon our long rope, slowly rolled out into the center of Gibbet Bay, hanging free over the water. We lowered the anchor until it splashed into the water next to the fore-rail of the sunken schooner, its rope scraping against a charred spar by the starboard main mast lift. Finally the rope went slack; our anchor lay on the bottom.

"What are you waiting for, Jeremy Albert?" Gerome David scolded.

I ran back around the cliff to the far tree, untied the rope, and then walked it back, careful to keep it from snagging on our dried camouflage or the cannons hidden behind it. When I returned, we tied the ends of the ropes together after passing one end through another wide pulley which was affixed to a tree atop the starboard cliff. Gerome David pulled hard, testing; the rope pulled easily but still grazed the charred spar.

"No swinging down while the line's fouled," Grandpa Barnaby said.

Using the ladder, we descended to the Trap. Father led us down the high steps to the Cave of Riches, and then down the lower steps to the water.

"Gerome, Jeremy; go search the cave," Father ordered. "Make sure that they didn't leave anything."

Pushing to be first, Gerome David and I hurried into the cave. We knew our way in the dark, but sunlight beamed in, illuminating most of the cave enough for us to see. The Cave of Riches was a round, stony tunnel twenty yards deep into the cliff behind the Silver

Sprinkle, just tall enough that our heads only brushed the roof. Looking carefully, we scanned every inch of the smooth, bracken-littered floor all the way back to the two weathered skeletons which had lain there since before we were born, the three empty chests, and the Skull-bottle, which we knew better than to touch. Gerome David and I found the few loose musketballs that we'd shot into the Cave of Riches, but nothing else. We pocketed them and hurried out into the sunlight, pushing and shoving.

"You're just a pesky mosquito that I like to squish," Gerome David teased.

"One taste of you and a mosquito would want to die," I shot back.

Salvage was hard, dangerous work, but the lure of finding treasures lightened our hearts. Grandpa Barnaby and Father swam out to the sunken ship first. With deep breaths they dove under, and minutes later they surfaced only to gasp air and dive again. By the time that they swam back, Margaret Blythe, Grandpa Jack, Olivia Frances, Kenneth Joel, and Cousin Sidney had joined us on the lower stone steps at the water's edge.

"How does it look?" Grandma Agnes shouted from atop the cliff as Grandpa Barnaby and Father, drenched, slogged up the stone steps.

"Mostly intact," Father shouted up at her, and he glanced at Cousin Sidney. "We'll have to blow 'er."

Cousin Sidney smiled; he loved blowing things up and took charge of storing all our powder barrels.

"The anchor landed aright," Grandpa Barnaby said to us. "Heave to, and be careful!"

"Treasure hunt!" Margaret Blythe cried and jumped, but Gerome David and I, not wasting our breaths, hit the water before she did.

Splashing, we raced to the anchor rope, which the adults atop the cliff had already started hauling to, making it course through the pulleys above and below. Gerome David pushed me aside to get first grip on the down-pulling rope, but I grabbed it only inches above him, and the long circular rope drug us quickly underwater. Gibbet Bay was four fathoms deep at low tide, nearly six at high tide, and halfway down we let go of the rope beside the sunken hull of The Scarlet Siren. Cannon-shattered, many of its timbers lay broken. As the rope drug Margaret Blythe down, Gerome David seized a broken timber blocking a large shattered window beside the anchor. I hurried to help him, but it wasn't until Margaret Blythe joined us that we pried the timber away and used it to break out the last of the window's glass so that we could safely enter.

By then, of course, our breaths were failing, so we pushed off the sunken hull, seized the anchor rope, and let it drag us to the surface. There, we each gasped a few times, and then grabbed the down-rope and let it drag us under again.

The ruined timber now removed, we swam through the open window into the fore caille officer's cabin by the cutwater. No bodies floated here, but the floor was littered with treasures. Margaret Blythe and I snatched up everything that we could, but Gerome David swam straight to a tall wardrobe and pulled it open. Inside it floated many fancy coats and other garments, each worth several silver coins. A huge, ornate wooden table stood in the center of the room, but we couldn't lift it; we'd have to winch it out after we removed the deck. Our arms full, we swam back out, grabbed the anchor line, and let it haul us back to the surface.

In the rowboat, Olivia Frances took our treasures; I'd gotten a compass, two daggers, a fork, and a pair of silver candelabras. Margaret Blythe had scavenged six books, but dropped one on the way up. We'd get it; by the time that we were finished, the sandy bottom of Gibbet Bay would be smooth and clean again, even the broken nails scavenged for Grandpa Jack's forge. Gerome David handed Olivia Frances a large wooden box chased with copper braces.

"What's in the box?" I asked.

"Couldn't open it, but it's heavy," Gerome David grinned, and he gasped deeply, grabbed the anchor rope, and splashed beneath the surface.

"Fragiles first!" Father shouted. "We can get the rest when we disassemble!"

Having sharked two more floating bodies, Uncle Rory and Cousin Sidney soon joined us in the watery depth, swimming into the broken hull through various doorways and cannon-opened holes, while Elviena Joan and Hunter Jack searched the deck, the only place where they were allowed to scavenge. Hunter Jack used his knife to cut through stubborn knots and scavenge all the rope. Salvage was dangerous; sunken ships leaned precariously and settled at unexpected times. We never swam upwards through a hole; if the ship rolled, then our only exit would be blocked, and more than one Wrecker had drowned by taking foolish risks. Still, it was our family's business, and with Father, Grandpa Barnaby, Grandpa Jack, and Kenneth Joel watching us, we knew they wouldn't be satisfied until no trace of a shipwreck remained.

"Keep a weather eye out for pirates!" Kenneth Joel shouted at me as I prepared to dive again.

"Aye, sir!" I shouted, and I gave him an affirmative nod and grin as I grabbed the anchor rope and let it drag me down. Kenneth Joel Wrecker was very old, Mother's father, still physically strong, but daft, easily riled, refused to let anyone call him 'Grandpa', and he was convinced that all of us lived on a man-'o-war christened Destiny's Ridge. He told great tales of living at sea and knew many lively sailors' chanteys, but we kids avoided him; occasionally he'd beat a child, accusing them of having derelicted an important duty, such as trimming imaginary sails or failing to scrub a non-existent deck. Still, his missing-tooth smiles were warm and friendly, and in a good mood he poured us stronger grog than our parents allowed.

I'd always dreamed of being a real pirate. Wreckers were pirates of a sort: land pirates. Real pirates sailed

the seas searching for prey. We lured our prey to us.
But real pirates got to visit distant shores; the only ship
that I'd ever floated on was our tiny rowboat, although
I'd stood on fishers, frigates, and twice on a man-'o-war,
but always while their ruined hulls lay on the bottom of
Gibbet Bay. But pirating was risky both for those who
sailed and Wreckers; Katherine Jill, Erica Nancy, and
my dear twin brother Chad Mathew had all died in the
last two years, Katherine Jill and Chad Mathew victims of
musketballs from sand-fleas. Erica Nancy had gotten her
foot wedged between some broken timbers when a
sunken hull rolled during a salvage; she'd drowned.
Grandpa Barnaby hadn't meant to be a sea pirate when
he'd left, but he'd found no other work in his
wanderings. He'd joined a rogue privateer only to save
himself from starvation, and then left it to return home.

I wondered what it'd be like to be an honest man.
Uncle Rory was the closest thing we had to an honest
man. He wasn't even a Wrecker; Uncle Rory McKeen
was the widower of Constance Gladys Hamlin.
Grandma Lydia had never been a true Wrecker, but a
Hamlin who'd married Kenneth Joel, and their youngest
daughter, Constance Gladys, married Grandma Lydia's
cousin, John Hamlin, a fisherman, so the Wrecker and
Hamlin families were twice joined. Constance Gladys
was then widowed when John Hamlin died of the fever,
and Grandpa Jack, before he became head of the
Wrecker clan, brought back Rory McKeen to be her
new husband. Uncle Rory was a strange man with a

funny accent; a Scottish scholar, and at his insistence every Wrecker child had learned their letters. Uncle Rory boasted that he'd never killed a man; deeply Christian, Rory refused to participate in waylays, and meekly farmed our small mountain-top gardens. I suspected that he would've left us after Constance Gladys died, but only true Wreckers were allowed to leave our clan. One misspoken word and the Royal Navy would descend upon us like Hammer and Fist.

I swam down onto the deck, saw Elviena Joan scavenging from the pockets of a dead sailor trapped under the fallen mizzenmast, Hunter Jack swimming back up with a thick coil of rope over each shoulder, and Gerome David vanishing down into the aft hull through Hammer's hole in the poop deck. I swam to a cabin door and pushed it open, then pulled myself inside. Light streamed into this cabin from two cannon-blasted holes in the ceiling, evidenced by the shattered pieces of timbers stabbed into the bedding and both floating corpses, one of which I had to push aside to enter the room. Ghastly, they floated in the underwater silence broken only by the muffled, bubbling swishes of my own paddling hands and kicking feet. One of the men, fancy-dressed, hung upside down by a wall, several large hunks of broken wooden planks stabbed into him, and a huge gap torn from one thigh, probably by the cannon ball itself.

I grimaced as I swam toward him. I didn't like dead men; their eyes always followed you and their ghosts

haunted Gibbet Bay by the hundreds. Yet I knew my
duty; after filching a pocket-watch from his vest, I lifted
his floating beard and hurriedly unfastened a gold
necklace, which bore an intricate tiny crucifix, pulled
several rings from his fingers, and pried a leather pouch
of money from his pocket, and then I spun over and
kicked against the wall, propelling myself toward the
door. I'd stayed too long and would have to waste
precious moments recovering before I could dive again.
Hand-over-hand I climbed as high as I could up the
outside door jam, and then I pushed off toward one of
the remaining masts and bounced from it to the surface.
I broke the water gasping and foundering like a
young'un, feeling foolish, but clutching my treasures.

"Jeremy!" Kenneth Joel shouted. "Look alive! Be
ye a lubber?"

I ignored him and swam toward Olivia Frances,
eager to deposit my treasures in the rowboat before the
others chastised me. Suddenly Margaret Blythe rose
high on the anchor rope with a cry of triumph, then
released it and splashed down, her dress spreading out
around her. In one hand she held three silver goblets,
and as Olivia Frances took them, Margaret Blythe pulled
five more out of her bodice.

"Real silver!" Margaret Blythe boasted, laughing at
me.

I held up my tiny gold crucifix and Margaret lost her
smile, splashed back to the anchor rope, and slipped
underwater.

I grabbed the anchor rope and let it pull me down, but descended only a fathom when the pull of the rope ceased, leaving me floating just underwater. Dimly, muted by the sounds of the distant surf in my water-clogged ears, three muffled booms cracked: *sharks!* I glanced about; Gerome David stood upon the deck, about to surface, but he jerked as he heard the familiar gunfire. He dropped his swag and pushed off, snatched up Elviena Joan, and drug her to the surface following Hunter Jack, who had started upwards at the first crack. Cousin Sidney and Uncle Rory, who'd been lifting something large out of the hold and was tying a winch-rope around it, dropped their prize and gestured for all of us to surface, but I pointed straight down; Margaret Blythe was somewhere inside the schooner. Again they gestured for me to rise and then they both swam madly for the cabins. I pulled myself hand-over-hand up the stationary anchor rope, quickly surfacing, just as another volley fired.

Crack! Crack! Crack!

"Jeremy!" Gerome David cried as he shoved Hunter Jack up into the rowboat, and then he reached for me. I was too big for him to lift but he tried, and then he followed me up into the boat only a second later. We tumbled atop each other into the rowboat, almost upsetting it, making Olivia Frances and Elviena Joan scream.

Something splashed about thirty feet from us as the thunder of muskets blasted again from the cliffs. I didn't see the fin but knew its tail: the shark jerked and thrashed, then turned and dove, gliding deep back toward the mouth of Gibbet Bay. Uncertain moments passed, and then cheers sounded. Regina Anne and Grandma Agnes lowered their muskets, Great Aunt Pearl still ramming a ball down a muzzle.

"It's leaving!" Grandma Agnes shouted down at us; they could see the shark far better from their vantage.

Moments later, Cousin Sidney, Uncle Rory, and Margaret Blythe splashed up beside us. Gerome David assured them that the shark had left, but Father ordered us ashore. They swam while Olivia Frances lifted the oar to paddle the rowboat in. Gerome David dove in and swam ahead, but I grabbed the other oar and helped row.

"Let's lift," Cousin Barnaby said, and Grandpa Jack agreed, still staring for sharks at the mouth of Gibbet Bay.

An hour later, all of the men struggled to crank the winch, which had one end tied to a main aft beam. The great ship, The Scarlet Siren, buoyed by the water, creaked and groaned and slowly stuck its rear up three feet above the waves. The main and fore masts snapped with resounding *cracks!* as the deck tilted; with its supporting ropes slashed and stolen by Hunter Jack, the masts couldn't stand on their own. The tall, noble masts, charred from the burned sails, splashed down on top of the fallen mizzen mast, their majesty nothing but ruined lumber destined to burn in our fireplace. We hefted our tools and headed down the ladder to the Trap.

Climbing out of our rowboat onto the raised aft, we set to work. We swung heavy mauls, careful not to hit each other, and the thin hull-boards cracked and shattered beneath our blows, sending wet splinters flying. We tossed the broken boards aside as we wrenched them free; few would float out of Gibbet Bay; we'd gather them leisurely after the dissection was done. Quickly the exposed section grew less and less. Gerome David found a lantern hanging from what had been a ceiling plank, but he tossed it into the water; this wasn't the time for collecting prizes. An hour after we'd descended with our tools, little was left above water but the main beam which our winch-rope was tied to. We headed back up the cliff to winch the ship a few feet higher.

All day this lasted, and still the vast bulk of the ship lay underwater. I wasn't surprised. Salvages lasted weeks, sometimes a month. There was little chance that we'd be seen or heard; Gibbet Bay was far from the shipping lanes, its mouth hidden inside a wide cleft, almost a bay itself, so the waves here were less. Undisturbed, we toiled day after day, slowly dismantling the ship a few feet at a time, sometimes using sharp axes, other times using great serrated saws. Our man-'o-war winch was the sturdiest ever made, yet it strained to lift the schooner's aft. Margaret Blythe took charge of the little winch, binding up the floating planks that we'd pulled free and making the other kids winch them to the top of the cliff, then pile them to dry. Margaret Blythe hated not being allowed to help dismantle the ship, but Mother insisted that it was men's work, and Father agreed. No one dove; half-dismantled ships often shifted and rocked from side to side.

When we could winch up enough of the ship, after we'd salvaged all that we could, Cousin Sidney lowered down a small barrel of gunpowder, and while we all hid inside the Cave of Riches, huge sections of the ship were blown apart, explosive seconds saving us days of work.

Three weeks later, when the last of The Scarlet Siren was winched to the surface and torn apart, the adults cheered and headed home. Upon the steps, before he left, Father nodded to us kids and we eagerly dove in. Gibbet Bay was shallowest near the Cave of Riches; we didn't need the anchor rope to reach the bottom here.

The adults bathed in the Silver Sprinkle, then carried our tools up to dry and grease, leaving Gerome David in charge. Kenneth Joel alone stood by the mouth of Gibbet Bay on Shark-watch, three muskets primed and ready. Gerome David sat down on the lower steps, his feet in the water, catching his breath. I joined him, tired from weeks of exertion. As brothers we often fought, but never during a salvage; Father would box our ears for squabbling while work awaited. The others dove in and recovered every prize that they could find to pile beside us.

After the excitement wore off, Gerome David ordered Elviena Joan and I to take over the small winch. We climbed the ladder and lowered down a rope with a large bag tied to it. Elviena Joan wasn't very big, but she was amazingly strong for her size, and soon we'd hauled up a full bag of everything from pistols and daggers to heavy cannon balls, both fired from us and scavenged from the dismantled schooner, even broken hinges and doorknobs. We unloaded our swag and winched the empty bag back down. Gerome David started rowing Margaret Blythe and Hunter Jack around Gibbet Bay, collecting all of the timbers; once all the floating wood was collected then the scavenging would go much faster. Over the next few days we switched chores often, while exchanging endless humorous insults, Gerome David putting me in charge while he took a hand at the winch, and soon we had a pile of lumber atop the cliff that dwarfed all of us kids. Hunter Jack cut himself badly on a sharp nail, so he got stuck hauling lumber away from the cliff to pile behind our house. The adults often came out to help, although they took more and longer breaks than we were allowed. Salvage lasted over a month, and only once did another shark discover Gibbet Bay, but Olivia Frances had been topside on Shark-watch, and Margaret Blythe and Elviena Joan manning the small winch, and they grabbed their loaded muskets, and the shark fled trailing its own blood.

A month and eight days after the waylay, Gibbet Bay again shined clean and empty. Father and Uncle Rory

carefully inspected the bottom while Cousin Sidney
boasted over his new kegs of gunpowder that he was
carefully drying out. Father and Uncle Rory found
nothing underwater but the sandy floor of Gibbet Bay,
and after we hoisted the anchor-stone back up, salvage
was over. The next waylay was set; while we'd been
lowering the anchor-stone at the start of the salvage,
Cousin Sidney had started cleaning out the cannons; a
few days later they were all primed, balls rammed, and
wooden cups secured over their priming holes, greasy
wax sealings around the cups and the cannon mouths to
protect them from bad weather, and their thick leather
jackets covering them all. With all of the adults helping,
Hammer had been winched up the cliff and rolled back
up its ramp, carefully-braced, and we'd piled new brush
before it. Under Grandma Lydia's careful supervision,
the younger kids had meticulously cleaned and oiled all
of our muskets and pistols, and Mother and Grandma
Lydia had reloaded and divided them back into our
swags.

The mighty schooner, The Scarlet Siren, with its
three tall masts, was drying firewood already piled
behind our house. All of its treasures were ours. Uncle
Rory was still caring for the books that we'd scavenged,
turning each damp page one at a time and rolling a thin,
perfectly-round stick across each, wringing out its last
drops of moisture. Great Aunt Pearl had three new
precious strands around her neck, one of black pearls.
Mother and Grandma Agnes had rinsed and dried the

grain that we'd scavenged, and a new slab of pork was roasting over our fireplace, sizzling and dripping grease into the greedy flames.

Our salvage was complete and we were ready for another waylay.

3

SEEDING THE LURE

"It's a crime to waste a chance for another waylay," Grandma Lydia said, raising her head off her new pillows.

"We have enough," Cousin Sidney said. "What will we do with more?"

"Store it for lean years," Grandma Lydia answered.

"Lean years?" Cousin Sydney laughed. "We've got four caves ...!"

"Enough!" Grandpa Barnaby cut off Cousin Sidney as our ears perked up. "You know better. Grandpa Jack, what do you say?"

"I say we troll the coast!" Kenneth Joel interjected, but no one minded him. We all turned to Grandpa Jack.

Grandpa Jack frowned, then glanced around at each of the adults, and I quietly sighed. Grandpa Jack was head of the Wrecker clan, strong, but annoyingly soft-spoken; often he took an hour to announce one decision.

"Another ... waylay," Grandpa Jack said slowly, each word a separate, heavily-exhaled breath. "The year's getting on. Few ships sail for treasure in winter. If we seed a map now, who knows when it'll come, if at all? Then what'll we do? In spring, do we seed another map? If we do, will two ships come, one during a salvage?"

No one interrupted Grandpa Jack, but everyone shifted and got comfortable. Grandpa Jack went on slowly asking questions that we all knew the answers to, but interrupting him would only further slow him down. Sometimes he could go on all night. Gerome David pushed a nine-man-morris board at me and I stuck a peg in one corner, then waited for him to make his first move.

"Still, another ship would help," Grandpa Jack said much later, his monotonous monologue creeping along unbroken save by the deep snores of Kenneth Joel, Mother, and the soft breathing of Devin Elliot, Edith Kim, and Chloe Gail, our three youngest, whom Grandpa Jack's low drone had quickly driven to sleep.

"Great-grandpa Zachary said that the Wrecker clan would someday own the world, if we could keep hidden and, one-by-one, draw every ship into Gibbet Bay. Our storage sheds are stuffed, but our woodpile is just enough to last. Another ship would let us build a big shed, with sturdy shelves, and stay warm all winter. Our roof's getting old, too; we'll need half a hull of undamaged timbers to re-roof it."

Grandpa Jack looked at his empty mug, then started to rise to refill it, but Grandma Agnes stepped forward with a full pitcher, forcing him to go on.

"Our numbers are what bothers me," Grandpa Jack confessed slowly. "We've suffered greatly in the last five years; not in thirty years has our clan been so small. We need a bigger clan, especially young women, but more men would help, too. The question is ... who will they marry?"

Margaret Blythe seethed a hissing scowl and turned away.

"Me," Gerome David said quickly, and he stood up.

Several chuckled, but others nodded solemnly.

"Aye, good boy, Gerome; its past time that you slept against the back-wall. Who else?"

"Margaret Blythe," Great Aunt Pearl said softly.

"No!" Margaret Blythe shouted, and she jumped up and slammed her fist on the table.

"Margaret Blythe, sit dow...!" Grandma Agnes started.

"Bloody Blythe!" Margaret Blythe shouted.

Uproar exploded, instantly awakening even the sleepiest dozer.

"I told you to never speak that name!" Mother's shrill voice pierced the tumult.

"The kids call me that!" Margaret Blythe retorted.

"You make us!" several kids screamed at her.

I grinned widely, the only smile in our house. Everyone was shouting, even those calling for silence, and no one was listening.

"Belay that bilge-water!" Kenneth Joel shouted. "Keep 'yer deadlights to the corsairs!"

"I'm not marrying!" Margaret Blythe shouted.

"You'll do as you're told!" Grandma Agnes screamed.

"I want a wife!" Gerome David roared.

A loud blast deafened us all. I, and many others, covered our ears as the painful echo reverberated. Uncle Rory stood silently by the front door, holding it slightly open, a smoking pistol in one hand. Utter silence and stunned expressions met his stare.

"I wish to verbalize and insist upon attention," Uncle Rory said firmly. He placed his spent-pistol upon a shelf and closed the door behind him. "As you have comprehended, since the death of my dear Constance Gladys, I've remained to cultivate and educate my children, however disinclined I am to waylays. I don't endorse the Wrecker family industry, but I concur: our clan diminishes annually. I'm tired of widowerhood. I will consent to a new spouse."

From the kid's bed, Devin Elliot and Edith Kim stared open-mouthed at their father. Many adults also looked shocked, but others nodded approvingly.

"I am unconcluded," Uncle Rory said. "Gerome David is past preparedness for matrimony. Miss Margaret Blythe is, in my opinion, neither prudent nor mature enough ... yet, but may be primly-primed by the time an apt suitor is located. Yet, there is another who, although presently unready, has their inevitable nuptial occasion nearing. I speak, of course, of Jeremy Albert."

A gasp burst from my lips. Everyone turned an appraising eye upon me; I wished that I could fade to invisible, but I only sat and stared, terror-struck.

"Logically, therefore," Uncle Rory continued, "since we can't leave Gibbet Bay undefended, I advocate the sole alternative: I shall pilot Gerome David and Jeremy Albert to sell a wagonload, find wives for each of us, and seek a future suitor for our reluctant adolescent bride."

After a confused moment, Margaret Blythe repeated her '*No!*' but it fell on deaf ears still trying to ascertain the meaning of Uncle Rory's brief speech. Through endless boring lessons, Uncle Rory McKeen had taught us kids that each word we utter defines our status and intellect, and he constantly urged us to mimic his fancy-talk. No one did, and right now I couldn't think of any word to say, common or eloquent.

"Duncan Barry?" Grandpa Jack called upon Father, needing no other words.

I turned and looked at Father, who stood with his arms crossed but beaming proudly.

"I approve," Father said clearly.

Many heads nodded, and smiles broke out. Gerome David swelled triumphantly as Margaret Blythe scowled; *Father had just married off all three of us.*

"I concur," Grandpa Barnaby said.

"Aye!" Grandma Agnes and Great Aunt Pearl chorused.

"Trim the topsails!" Kenneth Joel shouted.

"Very well," Grandpa Jack said with slow finality. "Tomorrow we load a wagon, and Rory McKeen shall lead our boys to their altars."

The silent shakes of my head went unheeded. Staggered, I stared as Margaret Blythe alone complained. Everyone else smiled and laughed, even the little children who had only the slightest idea that my future doom had just been declared. *A husband? Me? With a wife? Were they mad?*

Gerome David pulled me into a tight, brotherly embrace, his fist raised in triumph, and many cheered and clapped, but I hung limp in his grasp. A hand fell on my shoulder and squeezed; Uncle Rory nodded to me; I stared, ignorant of what he meant. Then Great Aunt Pearl hurried forward and hugged each of us in turn. A cold chill ran down my spine.

"I don't want a wife!"

Father stood before me in the yellow moonlight looking down at Gibbet Bay, the twinkling stars reflecting off its frothing seawater. We seldom watched Gibbet Bay in the moonlight for fear that its ghosts might follow us home.

"No man wants a wife," Father said, "not unless he's a fool."

"Gerome David does," I commented.

Father grinned and shook his head; I couldn't help but smile.

"It's children that we need," Father said. "Grandpa Jack Benjamin and Grandpa Barnaby won't be around ten years from now, and you and your brother can't waylay alone. By then even little Devin Elliot will be a shooter, if we all live, and Cousin Sidney, Rory, and I will run the household, but we can't do it alone. Remember that man-'o-war that we let in-and-out without a waylay two years ago? There were three hundred men on that ship; we could never prevail against that. Grandpa Barnaby's to blame: if he'd stayed here and raised kids then the Wrecker clan would be much bigger, but he had to run off and become a pirate for twenty years.

"Besides, even if you aren't ready now, in a few years you'll be like your brother, demanding a wife. Why wait? You'll be ready soon enough, and it won't hurt to hurry things along. Cousin Sidney will be wed to Regina Anne by the time that you get back; neither's happy about the union, but they're not related by blood, and the family needs it."

The next morning I was the last kid out of bed. Everybody seemed excited; Pearl made us an exceptional breakfast with cinnamon that we'd scavenged from a previous waylay but she'd insisted on saving for something special. Father said no more about my opposition to marriage, but spent the morning helping load our wagon. Uncle Rory got old Nicholas out of his stable and hitched him up while I wandered, trying to stay out of sight. I didn't feel like working, and everyone's infuriating smiles only darkened my mood. I slipped along the port trail until I could look down into empty Gibbet Bay. I'd dreamed of going adventuring all my life, but the prospect of suffering a wife twisted my stomach. I stepped to the edge of the cliff and stared out; long ago I'd jumped off this ledge first, before Gerome David, but only feet-first; Gerome David had dived in head-first before I did. We'd both gotten punished; no one was allowed to jump off the cliff, not even from the Trap. We'd all done it, of course, and gotten beaten for it, when caught.

No one was watching. I glanced all around, and then sucked in a deep breath and dove.

"How did you get all wet?" Mother demanded, and Grandma Agnes Laura came over to glare and frown.

"Ummm ... I washed," I lied.

"In your clothes?" Mother asked shrewdly, but Grandpa Barnaby interceded.

"Leave him be," Grandpa Barnaby waved them back. "Jeremy Albert's leaving a boy, but he'll come back a married man."

Reluctantly, with suspicious glares, Mother and Grandma Agnes relented. Grandpa Barnaby pulled out a newly-scavenged comb and ran it through my wet hair.

"A good woman cares what you look like," Grandpa Barnaby said quietly as he combed my drenched locks. "Uncle Rory will find you a good woman, but it'll be up to you to make a good wife out of her. The nicer you are to her, the easier that'll be. Just remember: your true loyalty lies with Grandpa Jack and the Wrecker clan; no other, man or woman, ever usurps family."

I nodded, although still frowning.

Satisfied with my straight hair, Grandpa Barnaby tucked the comb into my pocket then patted my shoulder and walked away. I felt like a bilge-rat, worse because everyone expected me to be happy while I secretly regretted doing my duty. I looked at my plain, wet clothes and wondered why they wouldn't let me wear any fancy garb; I was wearing a drab burgundy coat with a frilly white shirt, tight knee-length trousers, and red stockings. Aboard the wagon I had a dark green cloak. Many, especially noblemen and pirates, wore far brighter colors, and I worried about going out into the real world underdressed. Gerome David wore a dark, faded-blue coat, dreary even compared to mine. Uncle Rory was wearing nothing but a brown leather jacket over a bright red vest and stained tan trousers that Great Aunt Pearl would've used as a kitchen rag. I could only assume that they figured no one would notice us if we looked really poor.

An hour later, we started down the hill, almost the whole clan with us. Alone, Old Nicholas couldn't manage a fully-loaded wagon; the steep cliff-side road wound down for three miles before it reached the flatlands, and the wagon was piled with six four-inch cannons and a ton of other pillage. Hunter Jack was given the reins while the rest of us pulled to keep the wagon from pushing poor old Nicholas off the cliff as he neighed in fearful protest. Hours later, after we reached the flats, the long good-byes began again, but Uncle Rory insisted that the day was passing and, after an unwanted barrage of hugs, kisses, and well-wishes, Gerome David and I joined him on the wagon and we rode off.

Excitement levered aside my disgust as we finally rode away, watching the entire clan turn to walk back up the long road toward our house. I'd seldom been down to the flats, which were really low rolling hills, unlike the rugged mountain cliff that we lived on. Soon enough I'd be back, but at least I'd get to see some of the world before I was shackled to a wife.

Gulls flew high over our heads; a bad sign: gulls ate from the sea and came inland only when a storm was coming, but the sky was bright blue, mostly clear, and neither Uncle Rory nor Gerome David seemed worried, so I didn't mention it. An hour after we'd left the clan, we emerged from the low, rocky hills onto the main road, and then into flat farmlands where many people worked in wide, cultivated fields. I stared amazed; I'd never seen living folk who weren't fleas or family. Most were old men, but some were kids, my age and younger. Some were women, and I pulled up my traveling cloak to hide my face in case one of them wanted to be my wife.

"There's a cute one ...," Gerome David grinned.

"No," Uncle Rory cut him off. "No wives from neighbors; their relations would seek frequent social calls and inquire what industry the Wrecker clan employs. Besides, no local women would acquiesce; these farmers believe us a family of inbred mountain-madmen, and Grandpa Jack has labored diligently to entrench that opinion. We used to shoot at fishing boats that sailed too near, though we avoided hitting them. We'll be driving for some days past numerous cities ere we reach a seaport where we can purchase wives. Until then, assent to me all talking to strangers, and for your lives, never reveal that we're Wreckers; many would slaughter us just for the suspicion."

The garments that these people wore shocked me; Wreckers never wore rags. Some farmers actually had holes in their clothes, ragged edges, and almost no color at all. Only the poorest pirates wore nothing but rags, and our appearance seemed to startle them just as much;

these people stared at us as if they'd never seen a captain's coat.

Gerome David opened a bottle of strong grog and passed it back and forth as we rode past patchwork-colored farms. Kids were playing in their fields; our mountaintop lawns were too small to run in, and we'd get punished, if caught in the garden. They laughed as they chased each other; I'd like to have joined them, but we stopped only to water old Nicholas, and we slept in wooded thickets where we wouldn't be seen. Several farmers hailed us, but Uncle Rory blatantly rode past them as if they didn't exist. I stared at those farmers, noting the offense that they took at being disregarded. They stared angrily at our loaded wagon, trying to perceive our cargo, which was hidden beneath blankets, lashed down Bristol-fashion. All of the farmers wore strange clothes, different from the garments of common sailors or gentry; plain, mostly gray and beige, and almost always coarse and raggedy. Mother and Great Aunt Pearl would punish us for dressing in rags.

A strange figure stood still and rigid among the tall crops in a distant field.

"Who's that?" I asked.

"That's a dummy, you dummy!" Gerome David laughed.

"It's called a scarecrow," Uncle Rory said. "Farmers set them up to frighten the birds away from their crops."

I stared at the figure until I could see its painted face and straw tufts instead of hands. I shook my head; the lowlands held much that I didn't know.

Hard-tack was our dinner, crusty biscuits accompanied by thin strips of dried mutton. Rain and evening fell together; we threw a wool blanket over old Nicholas and camped sheltered in the dry space under our wagon. Several more days passed, us riding from dawn to dusk. Even Gerome David stared amazed; we rode past more people than all of the sailors that we'd ever slain. City people were vastly different from farmers; they smiled more, and some dressed in garb as impressive as our captain's coats, if not as brightly colored. Many were women, and I couldn't believe the variety or beauty of them; no ship that we'd ever waylaid had women aboard, so the only women that I'd ever seen were relatives. Uncle Rory began to acknowledge the strangers as we passed, and even spoke to a few, claiming that we were from some village called Clanth, that he later confessed to having made up. No one spoke to Gerome David or I, and Uncle Rory said that it was best as we weren't used to talking to strangers; one wrong word could get us killed.

Unbeknownst to us, among our wagonload of plunder was a large bible, secreted between the cannons, and the bible contained a folded treasure map.

"But I thought it was too late in the year!" I said when Uncle Rory revealed this.

"Don't fret," Uncle Rory said. "Grandpa Jack advised me to withhold the Lure until we rode homeward, and then to render it only to ship-bound sailors, else not at all. Thence we may hasten and return ere the waylay, if any occurs."

"Jeremy Albert can't help being afraid," Gerome David said.

"I was a year younger than you the first time I dove into Gibbet Bay," I retorted.

"You jumped; you didn't dive."

"I did both younger than you did."

One warm, starry evening, we came upon enough people to man a frigate gathered on a long grassy hillside. A wide, spotless sail had been hung from a taut rope between two tall trees. Behind the sail blazed a bright fire, illuminating the white sail as brightly as daylight. We tied our wagon to a fencepost and joined them, sitting upon the grass. A large man came out and spoke in a booming voice, promising us a 'fantastic magical apparition'. A puppeteer, Uncle Rory called him, but as we applauded, he only bowed deeply and then vanished behind the sail.

Suddenly, upon the taut, glowing sail appeared a great castle of many tall towers, in black silhouette, and a deep voice boomed out.

"Once upon a time, in a kingdom by the sea, the mighty Sir Glorificus returned from the wars, a great and honored hero."

Another shadowy figure appeared on the glowing sail, that of a tiny man wearing a high-plumed helmet astride a horse, his stark, crisp shadow moving bouncily across the glowing field of white. Uncle Rory and the gathered folk cheered at the appearance of this black spectral image as it floated stiltedly across the sail toward the castle.

"*Sir Glorificus arrived at the castle heralded by many great trumpets,*" the voice boomed, and the long, high note of a small horn sang out. "*The king came out to greet Sir Glorificus.*"

Another shadow of a tiny man wearing a tall, sharply-pointed crown appeared right outside the castle, only two feet tall, and when Sir Glorificus jumped off his horse and bowed to him, I noticed that both the knight and the king were the same size.

"*Tragic news!*" cried a high, whiney voice, and the figure of the king shook. "*While thou were'st away, winning wars for church and kingdom, a wicked sorcerer has stolen your young bride and vanished without a trace!*"

"*Fear not!*" spoke a proud, commanding voice seemingly coming from the shadowed knight. "*So great is my love for my blessed wife that none may conceal her!*"

"*And so Sir Glorificus knelt and prayed,*" the booming voice reported, "*and soon an angel came down from heaven.*"

As he spoke, the figure of Sir Glorificus lowered until his knees were hidden by the bottom of the glowing sail. Then, amid unusually loud strums of a small harp, the shadowy figure of an angel with great wings descended from the top of the sail and flew down to speak to Sir Glorificus.

"You can see the wire!" Gerome David whispered to us with a mischievous smile, but Uncle Rory scolded him with a malevolent hiss.

All evening we sat, amazed, watching as Sir Glorificus sought his stolen young bride across mountains and deserts, through deadly swamps, and over many lands, all of which magically appeared as crisp shadows upon the sail. Sir Glorificus was the bravest man that ever existed. Finally he reached the distant haunted castle that the angel had told him of, broke through its mighty gate, and cornered the evil sorcerer despite a horde of demons conjured to stop him, all of whom magically vanished as he waved his pope-blessed sword at them. The poor people of the land, freed from their enslavement by the evil sorcerer, cheered Sir Glorificus, and they gave him the castle and proclaimed him their king.

Everyone applauded. The puppeteer came out and bowed to tumultuous cheers, and people offered him many things, from old bottles of wine to live chickens, in gratitude for his performance. A line formed to shake his hand, and Uncle Rory let us stand in the line.

A tall, frowning boy standing in front of us turned around and stared at me, eyeing my clothes in the light of the glowing sail. His own clothes were better than most, clean and without holes, but still very plain. He seemed to take my fancier clothes as a personal affront and spoke very haughtily.

"I'm George, the miller's son. I've ground over a hundred bags of flour," he sneered.

"I'm Jeremy Albert," I said to George with an equally nasty tone, "and I've killed over fifty men."

Uncle Rory's hand struck the side of my head so hard that I staggered.

"No talking!" Uncle Rory ordered.

The next day, Gerome David did everything that he could to ruin the story of Sir Glorificus. He mocked and mimicked the puppeteer, whom Gerome David claimed had originated all of the voices that we'd heard, but to whom Uncle Rory had given a silver penny after the performance. Gerome David explained how the puppets were thin, flat wooden figures affixed to iron wires, and with his hand he showed how the puppeteer only had to turn the figure sideways to make their wide shadows 'magically vanish' from the glowing screen. I complained, but Gerome David didn't stop until Uncle Rory ordered him to be silent, far too late for my taste. Uncle Rory explained that he'd seen many similar nightly performances, and other types of puppets during the day, and even great plays where men put on fancy costumes and acted out the deeds of great heroes. My loathing for Gerome David grew, but my dislike for Uncle Rory diminished; I wished that I could see the magical plays that he spoke of.

Eleven days out from Gibbet Bay we rode into a great port city. Never had I believed the stories of houses stacked atop each other with ladders and stairs leading to upper floors, nor that hundreds of people lived together anyplace. Two days we ranged through a strange, crowded marketplace, Uncle Rory uncovering our wagon and displaying our goods to stingy merchants, most of whom refused to accept Uncle Rory's prices and offered only pittances in exchange, but slowly agreements were made, and our waylaid plunder was converted to bags of fresh carrots, asparagus, turnips, many bottles of wine, and several large barrels of grain. A few merchants exchanged us silver coins, especially for our four cannons, and by the end of our second day in the city, the only plunder that we had left was our clothes and the large bible containing our precious Lure to Gibbet Bay.

Gerome David and I were equally impressed; a winter's store of food filled our cart and coins filled Uncle Rory's purse, but that night Uncle Rory steered old Nicholas to a tall, steepled church, and left us with the cart while he went inside and asked for the priest. Gerome David beamed, but I sat fretting. Soon Uncle Rory emerged with a bald man clothed like a woman in a plain black dress. He wore a big wooden cross upon a silver chain around his neck; I wondered if we were supposed to steal it.

"Here they are," Uncle Rory said to the priest. "My sons, Gerome David McKeen and Jeremy Albert McKeen, the only heirs to my farm. Boys, stand up and show respect to Father Duncan."

Gerome David and I rose uncertainly upon the driving board. Gerome David bowed awkwardly, and I pathetically mirrored his movements. Gerome David started to talk but Uncle Rory snapped his fingers with a baleful stare, and neither of us dared open our mouths again.

"Three brides," Father Duncan murmured, staring at us appraisingly.

"Good women, undaunted by hard-living," Uncle Rory said.

"Ten silver pennies apiece," Father Duncan pronounced. "Thirty total ... and I should be able to find women seeking husbands. It may take a few days."

"Ten silver pennies today," Uncle Rory offered. "Ten additional upon worthy introductions, and the final ten for your services to marry us."

"I usually charge extra to marry," Father Duncan said.

"I may elect to offer supplementary coinage for brides of exceptional quality," Uncle Rory said. "But three we require ... and time presses."

Father Duncan reluctantly agreed. Uncle Rory counted out ten silver pennies, which Father Duncan heartily took, and then he vanished back inside his church. I stared at its huge wooden doors as Uncle Rory climbed back up onto our cart and Gerome David shook old Nicholas' reins. The freedom and excitement of our adventure had come to an end; Uncle Rory had bought us brides.

We spent the night in the countryside. Uncle Rory had bought some beef from a butcher, which we seldom got back home. We built a fire and feasted, roasting skewered chunks of sizzling meat on long, bark-stripped branches. Uncle Rory opened a bottle of blueberry-wine; I'd never tasted anything so sweet. Three days we camped in the woods, once riding back into town to see if Father Duncan had found our brides.

I took the opportunity to examine our Lure, sneaking it from its hiding place in the bible. It looked ancient, which was customary for paper scavenged from a waylay, then stained with tea, grease, and blood, and this map had one edge scorched by fire and had been crumpled and flattened many times, left out in the rain overnight, and then dried upon our hearth to give it the appearance of validity. It wasn't a map like most; our Lure was a series of drawings and ciphers with latitudinal and longitudinal markings revealing where the clues to Gibbet Bay could be found. The bottom drawing showed a full galleon anchored in an unmarked bay with a long ramp leading from its deck to the Cave of Riches, figures of men carrying chests overflowing with gold into the cave behind the Silver Sprinkle. Grandpa Zachary had devised this system so that no one could find the clues overland; only those who sailed up and down the coast could locate the secret coordinates to Gibbet Bay.

"Tomorrow's the day," Uncle Rory grinned as he emerged from the church into the dawn light. "Our brides will be here at noon."

"Beautiful?" Gerome David asked.

"I anticipate so," Uncle Rory said. "Father Duncan pledges that they're fine, pious, soft-spoken women of child-bearing maturity, neither too lean nor too portly, from excellent families, and of ages nearing our own. He reports that each has silky skin and all of their teeth, but we won't know further until tomorrow. Let's journey to the wharfs. Tonight we slumber in urban comfort; we have a bible to vend."

"You mean the Lure!" I grinned.

"That term shouldn't be spoken outside of Gibbet Bay," Uncle Rory scolded, his furrowed brows reminding me of his torturous reading lessons, and Gerome David punched my arm reprovingly. "Now we face the most perilous jeopardy of our journey, our very existence wagered, and neither of you shall speak again until we return to the road."

"I didn't say anything!" Gerome David complained, but at a glare from Uncle Rory he fell into a disgruntled silence.

Under the noon sun, many-flagged masts towered over our heads as we drove old Nicholas past countless docked ships. I stared, wondering which would offer the best salvage, slightly bothered that any of these beautiful vessels might soon lie as ruined timbers beneath the blood-stained waters of Gibbet Bay. I read their names, greatly impressed: merchant-ships named Horizon Lost, The Gambler's Net, and Hope's Flame, fishing boats named The Lusty Cat, Marie's Joy, and Harry's Catch, and a frigate named The Eagle's Talon. I wondered what it'd be like to sail on one of them like Grandpa Barnaby, and resented that our family that would never let me go; I didn't want to be manacled to a wife and made into an adult, never to play again.

Uncle Rory left us outside while he went into a large tavern. A great ship sailed past us, a man-'o-war named The Twilight Avenger, trimmed with dark walnut, its masts a deeper brown than any other. It dwarfed all of the nearby ships, and at least fifty men were aloft in its rigging, lowering gigantic sails. Forty-six closed tyre ports lined three levels below decks, one just above the waterline; cannon ports, more than ringed the top of Gibbet Bay. Gerome David and I stared at it; only once had we helped waylay a fully-crewed man-'o-war, and more Wreckers had died that day than any other.

Half an hour later, Uncle Rory came out of the tavern with a small, weathered man missing one arm, a thick quilt piled over his shoulders. To our astonishment, Uncle Rory ordered us down off our cart, and then helped the one-armed man to mount onto our driving board. While we stood watching, the stranger drove off with our cart, save for our bible and a few small bags that Uncle Rory scavenged from the back before the stranger shook the reins. Old Nicholas gave us a surprised look, then plodded off down the street.

"What about our food?" Gerome David asked.

"He serves the tavern master," Uncle Rory assured us. "He's driving our cart to a trustworthy stable, and then he'll snooze on the driving board until morning. Come, let's go inside."

Gerome David pushed me aside to enter the tavern first; anxiously I followed. Grandpa Barnaby had told us great tales of the countless taverns that he'd stayed in, and while my worry for our precious cart and old Nicholas needled me, my excitement swelled. All my life I'd dreamed of visiting a real sailor's tavern.

After the clean, bright sunlight outside, the darkness within blinded me, and the stench was vile and overpowering, almost making me gag. Slowly I made out the flickering red lights of tiny oil lamps scattered about on several tables, which somehow lit only the tavern's center, leaving all its corners in deep shadow. The large shabby room was forested by thick, aged timbers, all blackened by smoke and stained by God-knows-what, barely supporting a cobweb-hidden ceiling. Several wooden posts bore deep cuts, as if from an axe or cutlass, and I stood taken aback, fearing that the sailors who'd scarred those beams might still be about. Thick

wooden tables, more hacked and scratched than the
rickety beams, lay end-to-end in three rows, with
benches more splintery than any we'd ever scavenged
from a ship. The whole tavern appeared to be
constructed of firewood.

Uncle Rory led us toward a far-corner table
wavering just inside the center's dim red light. The
splintery table tilted when we rested our arms on it.
Questioningly we looked up at Uncle Rory, but under
his stern glare, we said nothing.

A scraggly, unkempt sailor burst through the front
door followed by a crowd of seven swarthy wharf-rats,
one walking on a wooden leg with the support of a stout
cane. The unkempt sailor stumbled and cursed, and
several of his fellows laughed at him, but a sharp growl
snarled from the one-legged mariner, and they all fell
silent. They scuttled into the shadows in the far corner
to a darkness-hidden table. The unkempt sailor, who
looked like many of the ghastly corpses that we'd
sharked out of Gibbet Bay, stole one of the tiny,
wavering red lamps to their table, and they looked like
devils huddled close over their breath-flickered flame,
hissing their whispers like a basket of snakes.

A wide, heavy pitcher slammed onto the table
before us, startling Gerome David and I. We glanced
up at a tall, round man with a thick, gray walrus-
mustache and steely eyes, who dropped three mugs and
a plate of small loaves onto our table, and then took the
copper coins that Uncle Rory offered him before

hurrying over to the sailors, who cheered at his appearance.

"Pour," Uncle Rory nudged Gerome David, and he filled our wooden mugs. I grabbed one and started to drink, then noticed the deeply-bitten teeth-marks in my mug's rim. Disgusted, I held it out so that Uncle Rory could see it, but he glared daggers at me.

"Drink!" Uncle Rory hissed.

Reluctantly I obeyed. The bitter ale instantly burned my throat and made me choke and cough; never had I tasted anything this potent, yet I daren't refuse. I fortified myself and took another drink.

More sailors trickled in as the afternoon passed. Uncle Rory ordered the old man with the walrus-mustache to bring us butter with such a savage tone that I feared they'd quarrel, and later Uncle Rory demanded three bowls of thick, hot stew and a whole quarter of cheese with the same caustic tenor. To my surprise, the walrus-mustached man obeyed without even flinching, barely noticing Uncle Rory's acerbic snarls, as long as he kept receiving more coppers. Then, as we ate our stew, which was quite good, much thicker than Great Aunt Pearl's, Uncle Rory reached into our bags, which we'd stashed next to our feet, and pulled out our big, heavy bible. He set it on the table beside his arm, in clear view, and the first scummy, ragged salt to walk past our table paused to glance at it before shuffling on.

As seedy patrons entered and exited through the briefly-opened door, I glimpsed the failing daylight outside. I sat in silence, trying to spy everything that I could despite Uncle Rory's command to keep my eyes on my ale. The strange ale tasted sour and green, as if brewed with too much yeast and not enough sugar, but its exceptional strength soon relaxed my mind in a swirl of blessed blurriness. Gerome David must've gotten equally intoxicated, for when one sailor fled out the door as a bigger sailor angrily cursed him, Gerome David laughed loudly. Instantly Uncle Rory drove his elbow into Gerome David's chest so hard that Gerome fell against our table, choking and gasping, doubled up in pain. Uncle Rory only took another sip of ale and sat staring at the scarred, filthy tabletop before him.

"A bible? In here?"

I glanced up to see a short, emaciated, long-bearded man with a bald pate wearing an overly-large blue vest brightly trimmed with badly-dyed yellow cord.

"Begad, ye pox-scurvy swab," his dark-tanned companion snapped. "Leave be what's none of yer business. Leave these sutlers to splice the mainbrace."

Uncle Rory glared up at the sailors before they turned away, and to my disbelieving ears, a barely audible whisper escaped his lips.

"Have a grog, old salts, if you're hearty."

Eyes alighted, the two sailors stared at Uncle Rory, who lifted our refilled pitcher as both swabs greedily held out their mugs. Uncle Rory poured, and then gestured for them to sit opposite us. Exchanging glances full of warning, the sailor in the blue vest and his ragged companion scooted onto the bench opposite us.

"I'm Rory," Uncle Rory introduced himself. "These are my boys. They're too big to stay a'bed and eating me out of house and home, ready for their first masts. I'm trolling for gossip on the ships and capt'ns here 'bouts, looking to quarter 'em good."

Both sailors glanced at us with wary, appraising stares, and then began spewing countless names of ships and captains amid reports of high-quality and declarations of skill, sturdiness, and generosity, which even my inexperience recognized as lies. Uncle Rory often interrupted as they blathered unceasingly, asking obvious questions, his preference for gold-worthy words cast aside for slangs and curses such as these sailors spoke so expertly that I'd have guessed Rory for a buccaneer. Long he let them ramble as Gerome David and I clung to every word that our ale-soddened brains could grasp from their thick accents and many exotic phrases, whose meanings we could only guess at.

It was the best night of our lives. We'd both dreamed of sitting in a swarthy, sailor-packed tavern, drinking and laughing, like Grandpa Barnaby had done. These were real pirates, I was sure, probably rich from plunder and ransom. Yet, as they talked, both sailors, especially the one in the blue vest, kept glancing at the bible.

"It's for sale," Uncle Rory finally said, and he half-pulled open the bible, then let the pages bristle past his fingers. "In good shape; I traded a usable pistol for it, knowing it was worth more."

"Aye, well-traded," the blue-vested sailor nodded appreciatively.

"Avast, what need you with a bible?" his ragged companion scowled at him. "A wasted life of drink and whores can't be sponged by holy pages. No rewards are earned by sinner's ways."

"Bibles can prop open otherwise-closed gates, and even a lubber can squeeze through a crack if no one's watching, and sneak in where he don't deserve."

"Blimey, you fool, drunken flail-bait," the tall sailor scoffed.

"Ten silvers is a small bet for a saved soul," Uncle Rory offered.

Two mugs of ale later, much subdued, Uncle Rory had been talked down to half of his asking price, and seemed to be nodding toward drunken sleep, before he exchanged the heavy bible for five shiny coins. I smiled, then quickly frowned, fearing a beating like Gerome David had received. The two pirates drained their mugs, rose with many a benediction for our best fortunes, and then both of them moved to another table, the short, scurvy rat in the blue vest clutching his heavy doorstop to salvation. Uncle Rory watched them go, then turned to us with a stare as sober as church.

"Time for bed," he whispered. "We're done here, and tomorrow's a busy day."

"That was rum-bucko!" Gerome David exclaimed, and Uncle Rory grinned and winked at him.

"Aye!" I agreed heartily.

"Get our bags," Uncle Rory said. "We've a room on the second floor."

We rose, Gerome David and I rather unsteadily, and drunkenly followed Uncle Rory toward the stairs, clutching our bulging sacks through the crowded, shadowed, noisy tavern. Gerome David staggered into me, then caught himself, and grinned stupidly.

"We did it!" Gerome David whispered to me.

"Aye!" I agreed. "Our treasure map's as good as ...!"

The shocked expression on Gerome David's face stopped me dead, and suddenly I realized that I'd killed us all. Uncle Rory shouted inarticulately, reached back, grabbed my shirt, and dragged me forward with the strength of Jack Ketch pulling a noose tight around my neck. Up the stairs he forcefully shoved me, and to my horror, many a dark-weathered eye stared upwards as we ascended.

That night, long after dark, Hell descended upon us. Our locked door suddenly smashed open and explosions deafened us. Men hidden by darkness charged inside, and something hard struck my head.

Jay Palmer

4

PIRATES AND MADMEN

Cold splashed onto my unconscious face. Delirium spun my wet head amid a chorus of evil laughter. Countless pains stabbed; barely I recalled the sudden crashing of our thin door, two blinding pistol-blasts, and loud cries of pain. I'd struggled in the dark against someone hitting me, but my world had unexpectedly blacked out. Now my world tilted crazily against violent jerks from behind that yanked my head up and choked my throat with my tight, drenched collar.

"Wake up! Wake up or I'll flog the lot of 'ya!"

I pried my eyes open against a brilliant glare. A wooden floor heaved beneath me. Strange, dark figures stood beneath billowing white sails. Past these figures, tall masts tilted as the deck rocked back and forth; *I was on a ship.*

"Leave ... leave them be," croaked a hoarse, familiar voice.

Uncle Rory knelt beside me, dripping blood from a bleeding gash that ran up his forehead into his hairline, wearily staring up at the dark figures. Bruises covered his reddened, swollen face with discolored blue and black braised patches. Uncle Rory gasped in pain, anguish heaving with each strained breath.

"Wake him up!" the angry voice cried.

"He's out, sir," a second, squeaky voice answered. "Shot: he won't last long."

Released by hands upholding him, Gerome David collapsed unconscious onto the deck, limp as a dead eel, smashing his face as he fell, and not-flinching from the impact.

"No!" I cried, but a harsh yank at my collar choked me back, evoking more haunted laughter.

"So, the tadpole has teeth," chuckled the deep voice. "Maybe he'll loosen his tongue ... with a little persuasion."

The dark figures coalesced to my deepest fear: *pirates, if I'd ever waylaid one.* Uncle Rory and I were shanghaied, kneeling before them, Gerome David unconscious on their deck. Three-score blackguards surrounded us, armed to the teeth, their belts stuffed with pistols, daggers, and long, naked cutlasses.

"He ... knows nothing," Uncle Rory gasped each ragged breath as if it cost him everything just to remain conscious.

"Liar!" the angry voice shouted.

I looked up to see a giant in a wide, plumed hat, clearly a head taller than most of his crew, his greasy, black-bearded face hidden in the shadow of his hat's broad brim, which was black but trimmed with gold and purple stitching, and looked new. A matching purple coat with gold trim covered his spotless white ruffled shirt, and his black pantaloons were tucked into huge brown boots, but his manicured attire contrasted with his filthy, disheveled appearance. His face was coarse, badly scarred, and dirty, and his black beard looked to be a tangle of mats. He glared at Uncle Rory, his weathered face flushed with fury. "You planted this treasure map in that bible ...! My men overheard the tadpole ...!"

"I told you, we ... traded for the bible ... and sold it hours later," Uncle Rory argued. "We never ... looked in it."

"He said ...!" the captain roared, pointing at me.

"He's a boy!" Uncle Rory gasped out. "I wanted to find a first-ship ... for my sons. They've been talking ... about ships and treasures ... all their lives."

"So, just a coincidence, is that it?" the captain bellowed, sarcasm brimming in his booming voice. "You expect me to believe ...?"

"Why would I trade a ... treasure map?" Uncle Rory demanded. "If I'd known ... treasure existed, I'd have gone after it ... myself."

"Aye, that's the sticking point," the captain growled. "It don't make sense. Tain't right."

"Maybe it's a false map," the squeaky voice suggested, and I looked up to see a thin, leering, seal-faced scoundrel in a long black-leather coat. His narrow eyes swept over me with an ingrained sneer.

"Why ...?" Uncle Rory gasped, and he coughed hard, convulsing. "Even a false map ... can be sold ... for a rum."

"Avast, a perplexing riddle," the captain scowled. "I don't like riddles. Here we got a strange map, and why should we follow it? What's this 'Cave of Riches'?"

"I ... don't know," Uncle Rory shuddered, and then he looked up at the captain again. "I never ... saw the map ... and I don't want to see it. Let us go ..."

The circle of pirates laughed, but their captain stood and stared, scratching his greasy, matted beard with sausage-thick fingers.

"I think not," their captain said at last. "Lock these two in the brig."

"Why?" asked the squeaky-voiced old man. "Kill them now!"

"No, keep 'em until their map checks out," the captain said. "If we find no treasure, and they're still alive, then we'll kill 'em good and slow. Stow 'em until then, in case we find some other puzzle that needs solving."

"What about the tadpole?"

"Tadpole teeth don't frighten: put him to work."

Hands grabbed me savagely, but Uncle Rory seized my arm tighter than any, and pulled me nose-to-nose, glaring hate into my face.

"Do as you're told, and none of your smart-mouth!" Uncle Rory seethed at me, and then a cudgel struck him from behind; he collapsed, and hands tore us apart.

"Rory!" I cried, but I was pulled one way, Uncle Rory another. Some pirates roughly lifted up Gerome David and followed those shoving Uncle Rory down the steps to the middle gun deck. Hopelessly I pulled to get free, and then I burst into tears, seeing the blood on the deck where Gerome David had lain.

Soon I was scrubbing Gerome David's blood off the deck, cleaning with a bucket of freshwater, a hard bar of soap, a large sponge, and a brush of thick cat-fur nailed to a wooden block. My ribs ached from where one pirate had kicked me, and my back was wet from others spitting on me. I ached to complain, but only trembled; I'd just get beaten or killed. Probing over my left ear, I found the cause of my headache; a tender lump the size of an egg protruded from my swollen scalp, and it felt hot to my cold, wet fingers.

Misery welled. *How could I have been so stupid?* I'd gotten drunk, careless, and said *'treasure map'* in a tavern full of pirates! Gerome David had been shot, was possibly dying! Small wonder that I'd always been treated like a child, mistrusted by adults, and never allowed out of Gibbet Bay.

"Put 'yer back into it!" a pirate shouted, and a leather flail slashed the air and cracked across my back. I screamed and fell, writhing on the deck; my back felt as if it'd been ripped apart. The blinding pain blotted out all thought.

"Up!" shouted the pirate, and the cursed flail lashed again.

I screamed; never had I imagined such pain.

"Belay that!" shouted a high-pitched voice. "Mind your orders!"

"He's slacking!"

"Kill him and you take his place!"

The pirate with the flail paused, then turned and stormed off. I looked up at my shrill-voiced rescuer. To my amazement, a bronze-skinned woman glared disgustedly down at me from under a purple-black leather hat. She stood tall, her bare, muscled-arms darkened by countless intricate tattoos. A sword-pommel shined over her left shoulder and three pistols and a cat-of-nine-tails stuck out from her wide brown belt, and she wore pants, not a dress, with tall boots that rose past her knees and had dagger-sheaths crudely sewn into their tops, each containing a long, thin blade. I stared flabbergasted; Margaret Blythe would love to dress like that.

"Back to work!" she barked.

I needed no further prompting than the agony of my back.

Few pirates bothered me after she appeared. Slowly I slid my bucket across the deck, scrubbing hard until I had no more water. Hesitantly I picked up my empty bucket and looked about, but all of the nearby pirates were busily ignoring me.

"Fill 're over there!" the squeaky-voiced old man barked.

As I looked, the thin, seal-faced scoundrel with narrow eyes pointed at a large barrel lashed in the fore. I hurried forward, turned the spigot, and filled my bucket, then spied his black leather coat beside me. His fist seized and yanked back my hair, twisting my neck until I was nose-to-nose with his snarling seal-face.

"If I was captain, you'd be spouting your secrets with a hot brand in yer flesh," he growled.

I said nothing, just trembled until he released me, pushing me over with a disgusted curse. He stomped away, and I hurried back to scrub more of the deck, hoping that no one else would notice me.

Hours later, my arms and back sore, I glanced at my bucket and startled; a face was reflected upon its water, but no boots stood before me. Then I heard a chuckle and a shadow fell over me. I spun around, seeing no source of the image, and then looked up into the grinning face of a strange, short man hanging upside-down right over me.

"Hello, Tadpole!" he beamed, and he handed down to me a large white seagull tail-feather tipped with black. "For luck!"

"T-t-thank you," I stammered, bewildered, as I took the solitary feather, my eyes glancing straight up. The man was effortlessly hanging from two ropes tied to the high rigging, carefully poised and expertly shifting so that he didn't swing as the ship rocked. He was the strangest man that I'd ever seen; he had the puffy cheeks of a newborn otter and the ruddy complexion of too much sun and windburn. Black locks streaked with gray stuck out from under his narrow-brimmed brown leather hat, which looked too small for him, but was tied securely onto his head by a leather cord knotted under his cleft chin, and decorated all around its brim with short feathers.

"Pope Captain Prince Tom-john the Blessed, at your service!" the upside-down pirate said jovially.

"Captain?" I asked, and then the oddity of his bizarre titles struck. "Pope?"

"Chosen by God!" Pope Captain Prince Tom-john the Blessed said.

Suddenly a loud, angry voice screeched: "Tom-john!"

The tall, muscled, tattooed woman charged forward with her cat-of-nine lashing viciously at Tom-john, but the upside-down pirate released one of his ropes and swung away from her, toward the rail. There he righted himself, standing on the edge of the ship, only his last rope keeping him from falling overboard.

"Angela, my love!" Tom-john cried delightedly.

His outburst seemed to infuriate her, but as she rushed at him again, screaming a high-pitched savage cry, Tom-john ran across the rail, jumped overboard, and swung out on his rope, inverted, and then righted himself in mid-air. His rope, as he flipped, wrapped around him, encircling his buttocks and one shoulder, and the effect lifted him higher. He swung across the deck over the heads of the laughing pirates, then snagged another rope and lifted himself even higher, and finally he scampered up a rope ladder until he was lost in the sheets. The pirate-woman, whom he'd called Angela, cursed him and the laughing pirates.

"Lubbers, I'll rip your backs open and wash the decks with yer maggoty entrails!" Angela shouted. "Tom-john, if I get my hands on you, I'll keel-haul you on a tight rope!"

The pirates quieted their laughter, but their brown-toothed smiles remained as Angela stormed back to me. She grabbed the seagull feather from my hand and threw it to the winds.

"Scrub that deck!"

"Yes, mad'm," I said, but I hesitated, looking up at the sheets. "What was that?"

"Tom-john," Angela almost spat his name. "Mad as a loon. Lives in the rigging. Won't come down for fear of my whip. Do you want to feel my whip?"

Instantly I splashed my cat-fur brush and swabbed. Angela stood over me for a moment, then wandered off.

Evening came in a miasma of exhaustion. My stomach cramped and my body ached; never had I worked so hard without food, not even during a salvage. Yet no one had ordered me to stop and I feared to get caught slacking.

As darkness fell, a rough hand suddenly reached from behind and cupped my mouth, smothering my startled cry. Then an arm with crushing strength wrapped around my waist and lifted me.

"Quiet!" Tom-john whispered, and he stuck another feather into my hair. "Spread your wings."

Tom-john glanced nervously about, then tossed me like a sack of wheat over his shoulder and ran to the mast. My new feather fell out of my hair, but I caught it before it blew away. As he reached the mast, his hands reached up farther than his height belied; Tom-john was a stout man with incredibly long, thick arms dangling from his squat-barrel chest, whose shoulders rippled with hard muscles beneath my clinging fingers. With dexterous confidence, he climbed the mast via a dangling rope ladder, as unbelievably quiet as an owl in flight. We ascended the mast almost as fast as I could dive into Gibbet Bay. The deck below us shrank as we rose; I watched it recede, staring down Tom-john's back. I clung tight; I was used to heights while standing on stone, not swaying on thin ropes and creaking masts.

At the forepeak we stopped, high up, though not even halfway to the top. Tom-john set me on a windy narrow shelf and I clung to the polished mast, which was more slender than one of my legs. About twenty feet below us lay a bone-breaking wooden deck ... if the swaying mast didn't toss us overboard.

"You looked tired," Tom-john said. "Wait here."

Tom-john grabbed a mast-bound rope, measured out seven arm-to-shoulder lengths, and then tied it tight around his waist. Without hesitation, he jumped sideways, grabbed a rope leading to mizzen mast, swung, jumped to a lower rope, and then he jumped free. He fell until the whipping rope tied around his waist snapped taut, and then he swung back down to land on the deck as if he did this every day. With quick, deft movements, he snatched up my bucket, soap, brush, and sponge, and then he swung on the rope tied around him to the fo'c'sle, then back to the shrouds, from where he dumped my wash-water overboard, and then he scaled the shrouds all the way back to me.

"Roberts would punish you for leaving this," Tom-john handed me my bucket with my soap, brush, and sponge stored inside it. "Never clutter a deck."

"Who's Roberts?" I asked.

"Mister Roberts," Tom-john scowled. "Dogwatch pilot."

"What's a dogwatch pilot?"

"Dogwatch is this time of evening," Tom-john explained. "The last hours before the sun sets. See? There's Roberts at the helm."

I glanced where he pointed; behind the mizzenmast stood the seal-faced old man holding the ship's great wheel. I ducked back behind the mast; how many times had I salvaged a wheel just like that?

"What if he sees me?" I asked.

"Ain't nothing that dog can do now," Tom-john chuckled. "He's a deck-crawler; never scales the sheets. He's been acting as first mate, but Captain Beckett hasn't officially promoted him yet. Don't worry; yer safe up here."

Clinging to the mast, I glanced at Tom-john's smiling face; how did he expect me to feel safe up here? Tom-john laughed as if hearing a joke, then reached up and unhooked a bucket that was hanging above my head.

"Have some grub," Tom-john said. "I seen you drinking at the scuttlebutt, but you haven't had a bite all day."

Inside the bucket was a long wooden spoon stuck into a thick, greasy stew. Even in the fading light it looked disgusting, but I was starving. I wolfed several bites, despite the horribly-burnt taste of overcooked vegetables in thick, aged broth; I hoped that it wouldn't make me sick.

"What's your name, Tadpole?"

"Jeremy Albert Wrec ..., I mean, just Jeremy."

"Just Jeremy? I like Tadpole better: has class."

"And you are ..."

"I told you ..."

"Pope Captain Prince Tom-john the Blessed?"

"That's right."

I stared at Tom-john, wondering if he was trying to fool me or simply mad.

"Pope?"

"Chosen by God!" Tom-john grinned, and he swung out, one hand barely holding a rope by the mast, his feet braced on the edge of the forepeak, with no more fear than had he been sitting on grass. Tom-john swept off his feathered-leather hat and bowed deeply, then snugged it back onto his head, its strap quickly in place. "Four times God has personally touched me; no pope in Rome can say as much."

"God ... touched you?"

"A mighty thumper God is," Tom-john avowed, and he crossed himself. "Reached down from his clouds and nearly killed me each time, but I stand still, although it sometimes takes me days to recover."

"Recover ...?"

"Haven't you seen them? God's fingers streaking white across the sky, booming thunder ...?"

"Lightning?" I asked. "You've been struck by lightning?"

"Four times!" Tom-john raised his fist in triumph, almost shouting. "That's why I live up here, in the rigging, to be close to God ..." Tom-john lowered his voice conspiratorially, "... in case he needs me."

I stared doubtfully as Tom-john gave me a knowing wink and then laughed out loud. My doubts vanished: Tom-john was utterly mad.

"Captain?" I asked.

"Captain of the sheets," Tom-john boasted. "Deck captains like our good Captain Colin Parry Beckett may choose our course, but no ship gets far without billows. I rule up here; these sails rise and fall at my command."

"Prince?" I asked warily.

"Prince of the birds," Tom-john said. "They're my royal subjects."

I absently shook my head; this pirate was insane, but I couldn't say so without risking being tossed off, and I could never navigate these ropes like Tom-john.

"Blessed?" I asked.

"Angela, my precious bride-to-be!"

"Angela? The woman ... with the cat-of-nine ... and tattoos?"

"God's most gentle creature, my beloved fiancé. Her love blesses me."

"She didn't sound loving ...!"

"That's just her way. She's the boson, the boatswain, master at arms; she delivers the captain's kisses."

"Kisses ...?"

"The gunner's daughter, lad, the tails o' the cat: flogging; a Jack Tar wench, me bonnie Angela!"

"She ... whips men?"

"Until they pass out ... and sometimes die," Tom-john grinned proudly. "God bless her sweet nature!"

Pirates ... and now a madman; my situation was worsening. I shivered uncomfortably.

"Cold?" Tom-john asked. "I can mend that."

Again Tom-john vanished, this time up a rope ladder tied to the main mast over my head, which he scaled with astounding agility. In seconds, he'd vanished into the evening's growing darkness. I glanced around; if I were careful, then I could probably climb down these ropes, but where would I go? I scanned the darkening horizons; if land was near, the setting sun hid it. The sea surged and the mast creaked as the wind pressed the sails. I clung to my tentative hold on my tiny perch.

Where was Uncle Rory and Gerome David?

Tom-john dropped down suddenly; in one hand he held two thick blankets, in the other a small, glowing lantern. He set the lit lantern between my feet and wrapped his blankets around me, trapping the lantern inside my blankets under my knees.

"That'll warm yer blood," Tom-john said. "Tomorrow I'll show you my kingdom, from the flying jib to the spanker."

"The front and back sails?"

"You've been a'ship before!"

"No, well, not afloat," I said, and to his sudden look of alarm, I quickly added, "There was a wreck ... near my house."

"Ah, a sad loss," Tom-john said, and he bowed respectfully. "No loss is greater than the death of a good ship. I should know; I've had three masts shot out from under me."

"Masts ... falling ... while you're up here?"

"Aye, a frightful waste. Criminal it is, killing off my kingdom, but shipwrights make new fleets; I'll never rest below deck."

"You live up here?"

"Shiver me timbers, it's a bucko life for a sea dog, handsomely!" Tom-john declared. "This is me home, a duty that the cowardly scalers flee in inclement weather when God's voice booms."

"You stay up here ... in storms?"

"That's why God chooses me ... for my bravery," Tom-john bragged. "That's why Captain Beckett lets me rule his sheets, and why my blessed Angela loves me: no man-jack's as brave as Pope Captain Prince Tom-john the Blessed!"

For my life, I didn't argue.

5

THE SEAHAWK

"Tadpole!" Captain Colin Parry Beckett shouted.

I startled awake, unable to move my arms, suddenly aware that I was bound with thin ropes. I cried out and struggled, but the cords held me tight.

"Belay that!" Tom-john cried. "Avast, Captain! I've scuttled the Tadpole to polish my masts."

The huge captain frowned, then turned away. I stared at Tom-john, who scurried down to me.

"Tied you myself," Tom-john smiled. "Takes time to get used to sleeping on a perch." He grabbed a loose end of the rope restraining me, tugged once, and the knot fell free, loosening my bindings. "Didn't want you falling off."

As I pushed free of the cords binding me to the mast, Tom-john held out my wooden bucket containing my sponge, brush, and soap.

"Can't believe that I slept up here," I said, looking down at the deck, dangerously far below.

"You were exhausted," Tom-john said. "For now, best if Captain Beckett sees you hard at work. Descend, fill that bucket, and start scrubbing the main mast from the deck up. Clean behind and around all the ropes. Do a good job. Breakfast will be waiting before you wash this high."

"B-b-but ... m-m-my b-brother ... and m-m-my uncle ...!"

"There's nothing that you can do for them below," Tom-john said warningly. "Your best bet's up here."

"How can I help them up here?"

Tom-john glanced behind him to make sure no one was listening, then lowered his voice to a whisper.

"Up here, you're closer to God."

A sliver of land gleamed on the starboard horizon, which meant that we were sailing north. I'd never seen Gibbet Bay from this far out to sea; I wondered if I'd spy it, but what good was seeing home? Like all Wrecker kids too young to shoot, I'd spent countless hours on flea-watch, scanning the ocean from dawn to dusk for ships sailing toward us. They'd see us as we sailed past, but we were too far out for them to recognize any single man, let alone a cousin scrubbing a mast.

Black stares came from the other pirates as I filled my bucket at the spigot, but I started scrubbing the main mast right at deck-level and slowly worked my way up.

Doubts kept needling me: should I be helping these pirates? What else could I do? I'd already proven that my judgment couldn't be trusted, but washing decks and masts couldn't help; I had to find Uncle Rory and Gerome David ... if they still lived. I was sure that I could find them; I'd swum through dozens of sunken hulls. But I couldn't seek them now; if I got caught wandering below, then I'd be punished or killed, and I was certain to be discovered. Insane as he was, Tom-john was right: my best chance to help Uncle Rory and Gerome David lay in the rigging.

The rope handle of my bucket over my arm, I slowly climbed up the mast-ladder, scrubbing all of the way around the thick wooden mast. The wood was finely sanded, newer and smoother than any of the masts that I'd sawn to fit in our fireplace. This was a new man-'o-war, three-masted and forty-two cannon: a formidable vessel. Normally Grandpa Jack wouldn't dare let the family waylay it because a vessel this size should hold at least two hundred men, which meant that the deck should be crowded at all times. I probably hadn't seen everybody but I'd seen only forty men and I suspected that I'd seen more than half. And these men weren't whole; many pirates limped or had recently-bandaged wounds; someone had waylaid this crew.

I considered telling them where Gibbet Bay was. Ship's cannons were great for sea-battles, shooting straight out at other ships, but most couldn't be aimed up at the high cliff-rims of Gibbet Bay. Aimed down, our cannons could pulverize this ship, and Hammer and Fist could penetrate any number of decks and hulls. If we sailed into Gibbet Bay, and Grandpa Jack signaled the attack, then even this mighty ship would be sunk ... and I'd be killed, too.

Tom-john fed me when I reached the forepeak; bread, bacon, and more of last night's stew, and then I continued scrubbing the mast, which narrowed as I climbed higher into the wind. The shrouds above the forepeak were twine-thin, a slender spider web reaching to the cap, above which reached only the stump, the pinnacle of the main mast, from which hung our pendant, a long, red and yellow striped banner-flag fluttering from the highest point of our ship. Frightened, I clung for my life; up so high, the pronounced sway of the ship constantly threatened to fling me overboard.

"Excellent!" Tom-john lauded, running a finger over a scrubbed section of main mast. "Now, attend the foremast, and then the mizzen."

Expecting nothing less, I carried my gear down to the deck, refilled my bucket, and started scrubbing the foremast from the deck up. The sun glared; it must be past noon. Seeing me, a few of the pirates scowled, but most ignored me. No more than fifteen men stood upon the deck. Mister Roberts stood watching several men repair a fishing net, his frown seeming permanently etched onto his snarling seal-face. The other pirates didn't pay much attention to him, meticulously retying the net's broken strands. Angela stood near the helm beside Captain Beckett, both examining an unfolded paper: our Lure, the map to Gibbet Bay. I wondered if we were heading to the first marker.

At the crowfoot, a small, wood-railed shelf on the foremast used for lookout, I found a blessing: six naked swords lay in the crowfoot, hidden beneath two thick coils of rope. I glanced to make sure that no one was watching, and then rattled one; only a loose cord bound these swords to the crowfoot. I made a mental note; now I knew where I could find a sword when I needed it, but what could I do, even with every weapon on this ship, against a crew of murderous pirates?

I kept washing the foremast, the spars and yard sail, all the way to the spindle, then descended and started on the mizzen mast. Standing beside the helm, Angela and Captain Beckett stared at me as I bent to scrub close to the deck, but I pretended not to notice them and dutifully attended my chore.

"Tadpole, tell the truth: where did this map come from?" Angela asked.

I stared up at her, biting back my rising bile. I couldn't appear nervous, but inside I quaked.

"I ... I don't know," I lied. "The bible?"

"Fool!" Captain Beckett cursed. "We know that it came from the bible!"

"You mentioned a treasure map in the tavern," Angela said. "Several shipmates overheard you."

"I ... I always wanted one," I said. "My Grandpa Barnaby used to tell us tales ..."

"He was a sailor?"

"A boson; a corsair."

"Who'd he sail with?"

"Captain Martinez, on The Seven Seas."

"Aye, that was his ship," Captain Beckett said, "but Captain Martinez's been dead for eight years."

"My grandpa will be sad to hear it."

"You better pray that this map is real, boy, or you won't live to tell him."

"What's this first marking, the drawing by the rocks?" Angela asked.

I started to explain, then caught myself; *I'd almost revealed everything!*

"I ... um, I never saw ... ummm ..."

I said nothing more, trembling beneath their dreadful stares, Captain Beckett with his black eyebrows as bushy and unkempt as his long hair and beard, though again immaculately dressed, and Angela with her beautiful, stern face, tattoos of ships, anchors, sextons, compasses, and great serpents twisting up her arms. I shrugged awkwardly, bent down and scrubbed the lower mizzen mast hard and thoroughly, hoping that they'd stop talking to me, but I couldn't help overhearing them.

"Look at him work," Angela said. "A pity that the rest of our crew isn't so diligent."

"*My crew!*" Captain Beckett snapped at her, but then his voice softened. "Aye, maybe we should keep him. What else can you do, boy? Ever scrape barnacles or hoist an anchor?"

I hesitated, looking up at them.

"I can master a winch," I said. "I can saw and chop wood. I can read and shoot."

"Shoot?" Captain Beckett asked. "Ever man a cannon?"

"No, sir, but I can put a musketball into a man at forty yards."

"A man?" Angela demanded. "When have you ever shot a man?"

I froze; what was I saying? What kind of fool was I? If I told them that we were Wreckers, then these pirates would kill us.

"It ... it was our ... our ... scarecrow."

Angela laughed derisively and Captain Beckett scowled.

"At least he can shoot," Angela said.

"Reading's a better skill than shooting," Captain Beckett said. "Can you read well?"

"Yes, sir."

Captain Beckett turned the Lure to face me. "What does this say?"

I stared; if I answered too quickly then they might suspect me, too slowly and they might think that I was lying to them.

"Those are numbers, sir; latitude and longitude markings, I'd say: fifty-one degrees ..."

With a sneer, Captain Beckett yanked back the Lure, preventing me from reading anymore.

"How 'bout it, Tadpole?" Angela asked sweetly, though sneering. "Want to be a privateer?"

"I - I'd have to ask my Uncle Rory," I said hopefully. "If I could just ..."

Their expressions warned me that I was treading a dangerous tack.

"Attend your duty, Tadpole," Captain Beckett growled, and I obeyed.

Next, Tom-john had me wash the bowsprit, a far more-dangerous task than scrubbing any of the masts. Just above the gold-painted lion-figure, the bowsprit bounced jarringly over the surf-pounded fore-keel. Upon the bowsprit hung the tiny yard sail, a comical miniature of the main mast, above which stood the jackstaff, from which our colors flew. British colors flapped against me as I cleaned the bowsprit, but these scoundrels undoubtedly had many flags and would hoist whichever flag they thought would draw the least attention. Every navy vessel was duty-bound to chase and sink any pirate ship, which was merciful: unlike Wreckers, navies took prisoners, at least long enough to hang them.

But capture meant that Uncle Rory, Gerome David, and I would die as well; I had to do something, but whatever I did, I was sure to do wrong.

I had to find Uncle Rory.

Below the bowsprit, great letters named our man-'o-war: *The Seahawk*. I grimaced at the ship's name, fearfully holding tighter than ever; falling from the high masts would've thrown me overboard or dropped me onto the hard deck. Falling from the bowsprit would plunge me into the frothing water right in front of the ship's splashing main stem, directly in our path. If the huge hull didn't crush me, then I'd be drug under, sliced apart by sharp barnacles, and left shredded in salt water to painfully drown. For my life, I clung tight to the damp ropes and tiny yards as I scrubbed the bowsprit.

At last my washing was done; Tom-john took my bucket, brush, and sponge, my bar of soap long used up, and stashed them in the crowfoot, and then brought out a small jar of grease and a tiny brush on a short stick. He showed me how to properly grease a pulley, using the slender brush to get in-between the wooden pulleys to their slender steel axels. With a deep sigh, I began all over again, scaling each mast, one at a time, crawling out onto their narrow spars, and then painting lubricant on the countless pulleys, large and small.

At dusk, as I descended the fore mast, Tom-john swung out over the rail and lowered himself over the edge of the ship, walking horizontally on the outside of the hull, just even with the capton. I hurried to the rail and leaned over, but Tom-john's rope hung inside the foremost middle tyre port where the gunners worked. A minute later, Tom-john leapt out of the gun port, his grip tight on the rope, and he walked up the side of the hull, his feet against the wood, until the ship tilted and he swung out free. Quickly he scaled to the rail near me, a covered bucket hung over each arm.

"Stew, bread, and fresh grog!" Tom-john beamed triumphantly. "Hurry, to the crowfoot!" Again he lowered his voice. "God may need us."

Amused, I scaled the rope ladder while Tom-john ascended on a leaping-spider's path that only he could climb. In the crowfoot, he handed me the first barrel, from which I pulled the bread, while he lifted the grog-bucket to his lips and drank deeply. I tore off a hunk of bread, which had gotten liberally dipped in stew as it was carried up; it tasted exactly like yesterday's dinner, and I suspected that it was. Tom-john set the grog bucket down and took the stew-bucket, using the spoon to shovel grub into his mouth. When we'd both eaten as much as we could, Tom-john lifted a large leather coat off the tiny rail.

"This's for you, matey. Zewdnesh says rain's in the air, if you've a nose to smell it, and he does. It'll be a cold night and you need to stay dry."

"Zewdnesh?"

"That's Zewdnesh," Tom-john said, pointing down to the deck. "Zewdnesh is the Ethiopian, the black man. He's a strange man; his name means 'Crown' in Amharic, which he speaks fluently. Some think that royal blood flows in him. Weather-master he is, the best on any ship; he hears God's voice."

I stared at him; Zewdnesh was very dark, old and wiry, lean but muscled. I'd seen plenty of black men before, but only down in Gibbet Bay during waylays and sharkings; I'd never spoken to one. Then I looked up at the sky; the clouds were white, not dark, but I knew how deceptive sea-weather could be.

"Can't we ... just this once ... go below?"

"Belay that crawler talk!" Tom-john scowled. "Hide from God? Tis' blasphemy! Now come; have a drink of grog, and I'll show you yer new home."

Drinking grog from a wooden bucket in the swaying crowfoot of a ship on rough seas proved more difficult than expected; it sloshed away, then splashed onto my face, but I handed it back smiling, though more grog wet my face than inside my mouth. It was for the best; Uncle Rory, Gerome David, and I would've been safely on our way home with our new brides if I hadn't drunk so much in the tavern.

Tom-john then took a lantern and led me back to the bowsprit, where he began instructing me on the tiny yard sail, how it was stowed and how to spread it so that it caught the most wind. He showed me how each line had to be carefully set, and pointed to identical lines on the foremast so that I'd understand. Tom-john may be crazy, but he knew everything about sails and rigging, how to carefully time each adjustment with the rock of the ship, how the sails steered the ship more than the rudder, and how different tautnesses billowed the sails, depending upon the speed of the wind. Never before had I understood the marvel that ship-builders planned more-carefully than any waylay. The rigging was a masterpiece of efficiency, sparse wherever weight could be spared, strong enough to withstand every wind that God himself didn't blow. Each rope and pulley was specifically made for its required duty, and the lines and shrouds held the masts together with greater precision than the most perfect spider web.

The day grew dark early, although evening hadn't set. The sky was black, the wind chill, before my lessons reached the mizzen mast. Tom-john hung his lantern on the brayles so that he could point out the unique details of the mizzen mast, but in the dark, his shadow on the mizzen sail caught my attention. Stark in the light of our bright lantern, Tom-john's shadow cast his figure in perfect relief on the taut sailcloth. I smiled, remembering Sir Glorificus and the shadow puppeteer, and stepped out onto the mizzen top, letting my shadow fall upon the sail beside his. I waved one arm, watching my shadow slide over the sheets, when Tom-john noticed my inattentiveness and laughed. Spurred by his humor, I pulled up the thick back collar of my borrowed leather coat over my head and held my arms in profile, scissoring them before me. My shadow became the head of some monstrous sea-creature, my arms in the wide sleeves made a great muzzle, and my scissoring shadows made immense jaws that opened and closed. I pointed my hands at each other to make sharp fangs, and when I bent to make my shadow snap upon Tom-john's shadow, he laughed and leapt away.

Laughing, I stepped toward him, wary of my balance, but he seized a rope and swung away, circling to the far side of the mast. I turned to attack him again, but he dropped below my reach, then climbed up the shrouds with a thin wooden slat in one hand. As I dipped my shadow to bite him, Tom-john whirled the slat like a steel sword, thrusting and parrying my imaginary attack.

"Back, leviathan!" Tom-john cried through a bursting smile, and his shadow-sword stabbed my sea-monster head, and I roared in imaginary pain.

Cheers rose from the deck; applause of pirates that I hadn't known were watching. I hesitated, but Tom-john seemed encouraged.

"Creature from the depths!" Tom-john shouted. "Sea-serpent! Kraken! Now you shall feel my steel!"

Tom-john swung back, and I turned to meet him, delighting to make my shadow as realistic as Sir Glorificus. I scissored my arms and shouted out a terrible roar.

"Get 'im, Tom-john!" several voices cried.

"Bite hard, kraken!" another shouted.

"What's going on here?" barked an angry voice.

Captain Beckett appeared on the deck below the mizzen mast, staring up at us, his glare lethal.

"Douse that light!" Captain Beckett shouted at us, and Tom-john hurried to close the lantern's shrouds. "Fool blaggards! Every ship to the horizon could see that glowing sail, and they'd be on us before we were even aware that they were there! Scuttle that nonsense, and you sea-rats: disperse! If you've time to lollygag then I'm sure that Angela can find ya work."

Not another sound came from the crew; the pirates quickly skedaddled. Captain Beckett gave us one last disgusted glance.

"Tom-john, no sleeping tonight; keep an eye out for sails."

"Aye, aye, Captain," Tom-john replied.

Captain Beckett stormed off through the door of the bulkhead and Tom-john and I glanced at each other, our smiles gone.

"You keep this lantern and sleep in the mizzen top," Tom-john said. "Hold it inside your coat to keep warm. I'll keep watch in the crowfoot."

Obediently I settled in the small mizzen top wedged between the tiny rails, the shuttered lantern between my feet, and my coat pulled down over it. Tom-john nodded approvingly, and then climbed down the shrouds with an expression so downcast that I wondered if he'd start crying. Soon I was alone, huddled in my voluminous leather coat, feeling ashamed. Again I'd proven how childish I could be.

Hours later, the cold rain finally began to fall, and I huddled close to my lantern, my collar pulled up over my head. I sat curled up inside my coat as if it were a leathery tent, when suddenly a thought struck me: Tom-john would never shirk his duty; he'd be in the crowfoot all night, and none of the other pirates would climb up here in the rain. I peered down; of what I could see of the deck, only two crewmen weren't sheltering inside the hull. Both remaining pirates stood beside the helm, steering the ship, silently getting rained on. It was deep night; everyone was asleep. No one was watching me; *if ever I'd have the chance to find Uncle Rory, this was it.*

I considered leaving my coat behind, but I might need its concealment. I carefully rose; the helmsmen weren't watching me, and the rain's splatters, gusting wind, and creak of the ship drowned out any noise that I made. Cautiously, terrified of slipping on wet lines, I scrambled across the wires to the main mast as I'd seen Tom-john do. Descending on the port shrouds, I stepped from the rail down to the deck, and then hurried into the shadow of the midship stairs. Descending, I found open doorways to the galley, from which a dim light glowed, and the middle gun deck a'midship, which was almost pitch black. I hurried down the stairs to the lower gun deck a'midship, which had a single lantern lighting it, but it was otherwise empty. Cannons, rams, balls, and kegs of powder stood unwatched, but useless to me. I felt very awkward; I'd visited here on many other ships, but always while swimming; walking these lower decks, not needing to hold my breath, was disorienting. Two more floors lay beneath me, but the next was the most dangerous: on the orlop deck were the gunner's, boatswain's, and carpenter's store houses, and many sailors slept there.

Where would they keep Uncle Rory and Gerome David? They could be anywhere, and I was sure to be spotted if I searched every room. *Would they lock them in a cabin?* Probably not; cabin space was scarce, highly-prized, and unlikely to be wasted on prisoners. I crept down the stairs into pure darkness filled with tremendous snores. Pirates surrounded me, sleeping in the dark, and only my shrouded lantern showed any glimpse of light at all. I didn't dare risk searching through these sleeping pirates to see if any were my kin, so I stepped down the last stair, all the way into the lower hold.

Pitch darkness met me, but I felt with my feet for the planks that I knew would be there, which ran the length of the lower hull. I tried not to breathe loud, listening as best I could for breathing, talking, any sound, the darkness so complete that I couldn't see my hand before my face. My hands touched upon, and I navigated by the feel of, great rectangular wooden boxes that filled the lower hull, but none blocked the center planks; sailors often had to traverse this section without light, so they were careful not to block their only path. Yet I found nothing.

Suddenly an indirect light flared: a ceiling hatchway opened. Light illuminated the fore ladder, and shifting shadows, footsteps, and whispered voices alerted me; someone was descending the fore ladder, and I was only ten feet from it. I slipped behind a large stack of crates, terrified. What would they do if they found me nosing around down here? What excuse could I give? I stepped behind a crate and shoved my covered lantern inside my leather coat and cowered down where I was, pulling my collar over my head, just peeking out of its gap as the other light grew.

To my horror, seven swarthy pirates, including a mean-looking midget, quietly scrambled down into the lower hull. Another man was so big that he could've been two men. One tall, filthy man carried a lantern and set it on the very crate that I was hiding behind.

"This's good enough," one pirate said.

"Keep 'yer voice down," another snarled. "We'll be hanged if they catch us together."

"Likely that rope's already awaiting us," said another voice. "As soon as they get more men then they won't need us anymore."

"Captain Angel said ..."

"Belay that, ya empty-pate!"

"*She* said to do nothing! Take orders, she said."

"Aye, what else can she say?"

"What she says ain't for you to question! She said for all of us to follow Captain Beckett, and she'll pay us for disobeying."

"Who said anything about disobeying?"

"You, ya rat; I seen them daggers in your eyes when you were ordered below."

"Tain't right! Captain Beckett broke the pact!"

"That ain't yer business, either."

"The Hell it ain't!"

"Perk yer ears and shut yer mouths! Angel ordered me to tell you to obey Beckett without a single complaint. She's got something planned ..."

"What could she have planned? They're watching her like hawks."

"That's why she ain't here, ya waterlogged float. That's all she said, and that ought'a be enough for the likes of you. We've never been in a worse situation, but trust Captain Angel; she'll get us out of here. Now back to your bunks before someone comes looking. We've risked too much already."

Some muttered grunts and complaints followed, but the shifting light on the inner hull told me that the pirates had taken their lantern and started back up the fore ladder. Then, just as the light was lifted through the trapdoor, a hoarse, weak voice wafted from the aft darkness.

"W-w-water! W-water!"

I froze: *Uncle Rory?* It didn't sound like him; never had I heard such agony in a voice. Yet the last of the seven pirates ignored him and scaled up the ladder, through the hatchway, and they closed the trapdoor, cutting off all trace of light. I scrambled from my hiding place and hurried aft, but kept my lantern hidden; if I'd searched there first then I'd have found them already, but was it them? Trapped in utter darkness, how could I tell? Who else would be down here?

"Uncle?" I whispered. "Uncle Rory?"

"Jeremy!" Uncle Rory's voice in the darkness was raspy, cracked and dry, but it was him. "Jeremy, stop! Go back ... get us water! Hurry!"

I rushed forward, holding one hand into blackness, desperate to find him. I held up my lantern and the glow from under its shrouds showed my beloved kin's familiar outline.

"Jeremy, get us water!" Uncle Rory wheezed, coughed dryly, and his hand suddenly seized my coat and shook me urgently. "Hurry! And bring a knife! Your brother's dying!"

Alarmed by his exigency, I stumbled back to the stairs. *Had they been down here the whole time, trapped in darkness, without food or drink, while I was playing shadow-puppets on the yards?*

I slipped up the stairs, found the lighted galley, and peeked inside. Several pirates were there, propped against the walls or stretched out on the benches. The galley was huge, but all eyes turned to me as I entered, my head as low as it would go against my bulky coat's collar.

"Water?" I asked meekly.

Most of them just stared, but one pirate motioned to the aft, and I followed his direction to a huge iron fireplace affixed to the main buttress. Beside it were many iron and copper pots dangling on hooks, swaying with the rocking of the ship, and beneath them were several stacked kegs. I found a large empty wooden pitcher, tried to wipe it clean with my fingers, and then filled it from a tap. It smelled like the grog that Tom-john had given me, but I didn't wait to look for another tap with all the pirates watching me. I spied a box filled with utensils; I absently rested one hand atop it, and after I closed the tap and started away, a slender knife was tucked inside my coat sleeve.

"The kraken's a tadpole again," one of the pirates sneered, but I ignored him and headed out. I couldn't afford problems now; *Gerome David was dying.*

"Here's grog," I said as I held out the pitcher.

Uncle Rory gulped deeply, long and hard. Finally he lowered the pitcher and coughed. He winced and shielded his eyes as I unshrouded my lantern, illuminating the dark hold. Huge crates and bulging bags glowed against the long running timbers of the dark hull, all pegged to the stout warship's frame. Uncle Rory's wrists were tightly bound, but he handed me back the pitcher and quickly knelt to examine Gerome David, who looked ghastly pale, unconscious, so badly wounded that they hadn't bothered binding him.

"Did ... did you get ... a knife?" he gasped hoarsely, holding out his bound wrists.

I set the pitcher on the floor and began carefully cutting his wrists free, one loop at a time, trying not to slice his forearms. A shudder ran up my spine; I'd thought that all of my problems would be over when I found Uncle Rory, but our problems were greater than

I'd thought. *So what if he was free? Where could we go, trapped on this ship of pirates?*

6

THE FIRST MARKER

I had to climb all the way back to the gunner's deck to fetch more lamps so that Uncle Rory could continue to treat Gerome David; from iron hooks between the cannons I stole four unattended lanterns and hurried back down.

"He's got a fever," Uncle Rory said. "That musketball's still in him; I've got to cut it out. Best to do it now. Hold him down and don't let him cry out."

My efforts were unneeded; the whole time that Uncle Rory cut and probed the deep, bleeding wound, Gerome David never flinched. His wound was in his upper chest, low on the left shoulder, and I struggled to hold back my bile as Uncle Rory cut deep. My brother's blood spewed onto all three of us; Gerome David had to be near death to not feel the deep slices and Uncle Rory's probing fingers, but finally Uncle Rory pulled out the bloody lead ball, which he pocketed. Then he thoroughly washed the wound with grog; the stinging alcohol affected no more reaction than the knife.

"Have they fed you at all?" I asked.

"They tied us up and left us," Uncle Rory whispered, his voice still weak and raspy, but better. "No food, no water ... how about you?"

"I'm working the shrouds ... well, cleaning and greasing ..."

"Good. Where are we?"

"Sailing north."

"To the first marker; they're following the Lure. Once they've got both markers, then they'll sail to Gibbet Bay: we'll be a flea-bag."

"Not if we tell them ..."

"Tell them nothing! One wrong word and we die."

"But the waylay will kill us!"

"Yes, yes, it will."

"What should I ...?"

"Do nothing. Obey every order that you're given. It takes most ships five days to follow the Lure, to get both coordinates and sail to Gibbet Bay. Being a man-'o-war, we can't be traveling faster than ten knots; that helps, but two days have already passed.

"Mind your business, and keep yourself alive. Don't do anything unless I tell you to: I'll decide how we escape, if at all. If only our deaths can save the family, then that's our duty. But I need food, water, and information. Keep your mouth shut but your ears open."

"I can get food," I said, "but I won't be able to bring it until tomorrow night."

"Good. Don't risk coming at all, if you might get caught. We've only got a few more days; if I can revive Gerome David, then we'll try and save him. If he dies, then you and I'll slip overboard and swim for shore."

"We're far out to sea."

"We'll have to risk it."

The stars were fading before I climbed back into my breezy, creaking perch. My lantern was out; I'd poured all of my oil into one of the lanterns that I'd left with Uncle Rory, since daylight would never reach the lower hull. I felt chilled and exhausted, but the rain had stopped. The sun's first rays beamed streamers of foreboding to the fading stars and pained my weary eyes.

"All hands on deck!"

I sat up, clutching my leather coat tightly around me. A moment later the tramp of feet reverberated throughout the ship.

"Aloft! Trim the sails!"

Pirates leapt to the ladders and shrouds. Tom-john appeared in the top armor, shouting orders.

"Mind the mainyard tackles! Together! Don't bunch the sheets!"

I joined them, crawling out onto the farthest end of the main yard, precariously balancing until I grasped the brace line. Each pirate obeyed Tom-john's orders without hesitation; he truly was captain up here. As they loosed the sails, I rapidly pulled up my end one-handed, unsuccessfully trying to match the speed of the pirate beside me, who balanced on the yard with ease and used both hands.

"Lubber!" he cursed as my slowness fouled his rapidity. "Look alive!"

"Both hands, Tadpole!" Tom-john ordered. "Lean back and lift in folds; don't bunch the sheet!"

Carefully I let go and used both hands, trying to do as ordered. The effort was surprisingly easy, once I leaned backwards to counterbalance pulling up the heavy sail. Quickly the other pirates folded their sections; mine came up much slower and folded less neatly. I was the last to tie up my end, precariously balancing as I knotted the last tie.

"There ... just like on the map," Mr. Roberts shouted, and half of the crew turned to follow the spyglass attached to his eye.

A hundred yards to starboard, half a mile from a bleak, rocky shore, seawater splashed against stony reefs. Dangerous points of gray rock stabbed up through the water's surface; a dozen pillars jutted ten feet above the waves, their lower halves soaked from the briny spray of the surf, which rose and fell against their bases, while others were only visible by the waves splashing over them. Rocks like these could tear a ship apart; I recognized these stones at once, although I'd never expected to see them. Every Lure that we'd ever drawn showed these familiar jutting stones: the first marker to Gibbet Bay.

"Take us in, but not too close!" Captain Beckett ordered. "Ready the jolly-boat!"

Four rowboats lay athwartships; the sailors winched one up and lifted it over the side as our ship drifted forward on its own momentum.

"Drop anchor!"

The clink-clanking of the anchor chain resounded loudly over the ocean's roar.

"Tadpole!"

I froze; Angela was on the forecastle, looking up at me.

"Tadpole, come here!" Angela ordered.

Alarmed, but knowing that I daren't refuse, I crossed the yard, then descended the ladder and approached Angela, who stood beside Captain Beckett, who was looking at her skeptically.

"Captain, Tadpole here can read, probably better than any of your rats," Angela said. "Why not send him along? Be a good test of his loyalty."

Captain Beckett glared at me, then nodded.

"Into the jolly, boy, and mind your duty," Captain Beckett said. "Mr. Roberts, lead the skiff. If Tadpole gives you any trouble ..."

"Gladly, Captain," Mr. Roberts promised, leering eagerly.

Mr. Roberts grabbed my arm and shoved me all the way to the rail. The pirates below were just unhooking their block-and-tackles, the pirates above pulling their ropes back up onto the deck. I scrambled down the freeboard on a Jacob's ladder, my worn boots pinched by every ratline. Mr. Roberts followed me down into the tiny boat, which was exactly like our rowboat back home, save that it had never been used for sharking.

"Push off!" Mr. Roberts barked like the seal he resembled. "Careful! If we hit them rocks then I'll skin yer hides!"

Every Lure started with the coordinates of these rocks with a picture of a rowboat holding position behind the biggest spire, right over the reef, where no large ship could sail. I'd always hoped to see it, but never as a prisoner.

"Put yer backs into it!"

Six men plied the oars with experienced precision. Mr. Roberts navigated us to the exact spot, carefully circling the biggest spire, while avoiding the many smaller rocks. The rise and fall of the water threatened to drop us on several hidden spires, but our rowers braced their oars against the rocks as we closed on their weathered edges, each outcropping a stony fang to splinter our tiny boat.

"There!" I cried, pointing. "Look!"

Upon the very surface of the tall spire of smooth rock, chiseled there by Zachary William Wrecker, founder of our clan, lay the longitudinal coordinate of

Gibbet Bay. I stared at my family's history, engraved a century ago, a monument to pirate ingenuity. No passing ship could see it, and it was too distant to be read from shore.

"Read it, boy, if you can," Mr. Roberts ordered.

"One degree, nineteen minutes east," I said.

"Aye, that's how I read it, too," Mr. Roberts said. "Take us back, ya dogs!"

Fifteen minutes later, I climbed over the gunwale and reported the longitudinal coordinate to Captain Beckett.

"Is that true, Mr. Roberts?"

"Aye, Captain."

"That's not far away," Captain Beckett snarled, "but it runs past long coastlines in two places. At least we found something; otherwise Tadpole would be showing us his guts. Let's find the latitude. Weigh anchor. Come about. Loose the sheets."

"Tadpole, resume your station," Angela said as Mr. Roberts shouted Captain Beckett's orders to the crew.

I hurried to the main mast, but a line of men were scrambling up, and I didn't dare push before them. The sheets were flying before my feet left the deck, other sailors hurrying to post the belaying pins, which bound the ship's rigging fast. The ship swayed mightily as we turned toward the second marker.

As soon as the sails were set, all of the sailors returned to the deck, but Tom-john and I remained above. I glanced at his smiling face, hesitantly speaking.

"Tom-john, I mean ..., Prince Captain Pope ... I can't remember the other ..."

"Pope Captain Prince ... the Blessed," Tom-john smiled. "What'cha want?"

"Can you teach me ... to be a real sailor?"

"Good lad!"

"I want to know everything. I know three knots: clove, bowline, and hitch ..."

"I know twenty-three sailor's knots, boy, including some that few sailors can untie."

"Twenty-three? How long have you been sailing?"

"Since I was twelve," Tom-john bragged. "Killed a man in my first week; a bonnie triumph, I tell you. You wouldn't know about that, being born of a respectable family, but for wharf-rats like me ..."

"Where were you born?"

"In the Three Skulls, my mother's brothel. Never knew my father; my mother thinks that she remembers his face, but she never caught his name nor ever saw him again. I grew up on the docks, and boarded the first ship that would take me."

"This ship?"

"No, The Manta Queen, sailed by Captain O'Brian, God rest his soul. I've sailed on four ships under six different captains: O'Brian, Turnley, Silver-tooth, Captain Corker, Angel, and Beckett."

"Angel?"

"Aye, Captain Angel; you know: Angela."

"Angela was a captain?"

"Begad, a great Jack Tar; Captain Angel we called her. Crafty as a dolphin; she thinks whirlpools around most men. She didn't captain long, but she was my most-profitable captain, and generous she was. Captain Angel, my bonnie beauty!"

"But ... why isn't she ..."

"Ah, lad, that's a harsh tale, and the bad blood's still fresh among the crew; you're best not mentioning it."

"How can I mention what I don't know? The crew hates me. Isn't it best ... that I know what not to say?"

"Aye," Tom-john considered, frowning and scratching his stubbly face. "Let's flight to the top; best these words be not overheard."

I climbed up behind Tom-john, thinking fast. Uncle Rory had told me to keep my ears open; he needed to know what was going on. We enmeshed ourselves in the narrow webbing of the upper shrouds below the flapping, colorful pendant, where the sway of the ship was greatest. I clung tight, still unused to the precarious height.

"It all started with these new man-'o-wars," Tom-john said once we settled on opposite sides of the thin mast far above the deck. "T'was a bad time for pirates. The French and British navies built these man-'o-wars, which boasted crews of three hundred, and drafted a third bigger than any of the frigates and schooners that we sailed. Many pirate ships were sunk, including Silver-tooth's, which I was on. For over a decade, we fled from every man-'o-war, but these ships are powerful-gunned and fast for their bulk. Soon only three great pirate captains remained, Captain Beckett, who always had the best reputation for treachery, Captain WhiskyJack, a thrice-blessed, crafty old salt who knew every pirate-trick, and Captain Angel, who'd only captained for two years, but had proven herself many times. She's an incredible strategist and boasted the most-loyal crew on any sea.

"Captain Angel devised the Pact, an agreement between all three pirate captains to join forces and commandeer one man-'o-war, and then use it to gain two more, so that each of the three pirate captains could have one of the mightiest ships afloat. Beckett, WhiskyJack, and Angel all swore oaths to the Pact.

"Planned by Captain Angel, we surrounded and came upon this man-'o-war, The Seahawk, by night. All three of our ships were spotted, but The Seahawk turned to broadside Captain WhiskyJack's ship first; they sank his noble frigate, Horizon Sinister, before he even got close. Sinking fast, Captain WhiskyJack's crew jumped overboard and swam for us, eager to swarm aboard and help us, while the Horizon Sinister floundered. Next, The Seahawk turned to batter Captain Beckett's ship, The Wicked Delight, as fast a schooner as you ever saw; it was mortally-wounded, and many crewmates were lost to cannon and ball, but never was there a more-determined captain than Beckett. Although wounded, The Wicked Delight pulled alongside and boarded: Captain Beckett's whole crew fought their way onto the fore. Captain Angel masterfully sailed our ship, The

Silver Enchantment, and boarded The Seahawk near its aft with only a few scratches and no losses. Both crews swarmed aboard. The Pact was working and the numbers were ours.

"But, against the Pact, Captain Beckett unexpectedly led his men below decks, where the tight confines protected them. Captain Beckett's pirates barricaded themselves inside the hull, meeting little resistance and suffering few losses, while we fought madly on deck, outnumbered three-to-one against men on deck and in the sheets. Most of our crew lay slaughtered at our feet, a dear cost, before Beckett the Blackguard led his men back onto deck to rescue us. Ambushed between us and Captain Beckett, their powder mostly spent, Captain Beckett paid them their final wages, but we nine are all that survived of Angela's men. The Seahawk was ours, but at great cost.

"By agreement of the Pact, each pirate captain had stuffed their ship with two hundred men; of those left alive on the captured Seahawk, Captain Angel had only fourteen left, five mortally-wounded, and Captain Beckett had only sixty-three, many wounded; only forty-two survived their wounds another week. Though his ship was lost, a hundred and fifty of Captain WhiskyJack's crew had survived by swimming away from the sinking Horizon Sinister. Many reached The Seahawk and called for lines, but Captain Beckett assumed command of The Seahawk and ordered his men to set sail. Captain Angel objected, but Captain

Beckett put a knife to her throat and forced her to submit; his crew outnumbered ours six-to-one.

"Left behind as we set sail, Captain WhiskyJack's hundred and fifty sailors turned and swam toward The Silver Enchantment, Captain Angel's abandoned ship, the only pirate ship that wasn't sinking, but Captain Beckett ordered The Seahawk to come about, and without warning, his men fired all our gunnage and sank The Silver Enchantment, Captain Angel's beautiful schooner; a tragic loss. Then we sailed away, stranding all one hundred and fifty of Captain WhiskyJack's men shipless in open sea, doomed to Davy Jones."

"Why didn't he save them?" I asked, appalled.

"Captain Beckett only commands The Seahawk because his crew outnumbers Captain Angel's. Captain Beckett broke the Pact; if he'd let Captain WhiskyJack's men aboard then he mightn't have been captain. We put into a safe port, but Captain Beckett only took on fifteen additional sailors, despite that this man-'o-war needs a crew of two hundred and fifty. Captain Beckett ordered his men to befriend the newcomers, insuring his captaincy.

"And that's our danger, although no one dares mention it: once Captain Beckett has enough men, will he keep Angela and us, her old crew, knowing that he betrayed us? Captain WhiskyJack and his crew can't avenge themselves, unless from Jones' Locker. Why should Captain Beckett leave us alive, whom he betrayed? Wise men don't spare the dog that bites, and Angela's teeth are sharp."

Amazed, I stared, trying not to let my expression reveal what I knew; this explained the strange meeting in the lower hull. Never had I guessed that those conspiring pirates had been Angela's! Now their words made sense, but why hadn't Tom-john been among them? Had he refused to descend so far inside the hull, or had they decided that Tom-john was too insane to invite? Should I tell him? Saying that I'd overheard his men would reveal that I'd been sneaking about; Tom-john may be crazy, but he wasn't stupid, and he seemed obedient to Captain Beckett. Which side would he be on if his old shipmates mutinied?

"What side should I ... we ...?"

"Lad, to you, these matters is death," Tom-john said. "I only told you so that you'd know why, if Captain Beckett suddenly chooses to kill us. But he may spare old Tom-john; no other sailor's as brave when God's fingers arc down from the sky, and you, well, you were never part of Angela's crew. We may be spared, though no happiness will I feel watching my friends die. Still: a pirate's life, eh? We knew the risks. My deadlights have spied many a worse betrayal back in the old days. Now, enough history; how about them knots?"

Tom-john pulled out a small coil of thin rope and showed me six knots that I'd never seen, including one that I spent ten minutes trying to untie, and never managed. I learned the first five knots that Tom-john showed me, but his mystery knot baffled me.

After dusk, Tom-john and I scaled down the outside of the hull to fetch fresh grog and food. The dark, close sea crashed just below us, spraying foam frighteningly close; if we fell, only the star-lit aft of the ship would be visible as it sailed away, leaving us to drown. But Tom-john taught me how to wrap the rope smartly about me, so I was tightly held, but not bound; in some cases, having the rope tied to you was more dangerous, Tom-john insisted. The rocking of the ship sometimes lifted us from its wet timbers, swinging us out, but then we'd crash back, all at regular intervals. Through a wide portal we got vittles and drinks from the cook, to whom Tom-john was formally polite and always referred to as *'Master Below Decks'*. The fat cook had a friendly face when he looked at Tom-john, but he eyed me suspiciously. He passed us grog and food through his kitchen porthole, and then we scurried back up to the crowfoot, where we shared a bonnie meal, laughing uncontrollably at the slightest jest. We played a little shadow-puppets with our tiny lantern, making shapes with our hands upon a tiny section of the sail, making only small shapes; Tom-john didn't want Captain Beckett angry at him again, and I shared his fears. Tom-john made incredibly-realistic shapes with his hands: shadows of ducks, dogs, and many kinds of fish. He taught me how, and we spent a pleasant evening in the small glow of our lantern, drinking grog and laughing. I'd never had a real friend before; Tom-john was almost like having my dear brother, Chad Mathew, back again.

Early, I faked several yawns, and Tom-john left me to sleep while he climbed the main mast to keep watch. I curled up on the crowfoot between the tiny rails, now quite used to sleeping aloft, my blanket and heavy leather coat wrapped tightly around me so that the wind wouldn't blow either overboard, and I kept the lantern inside my covers to keep warm, but I daren't fall asleep. Our bucket still had plenty of stew left in it, and I needed to get it to Uncle Rory as soon as the crew began to slumber.

When no movement showed, I closed the shrouds on my lantern, slipped out of my blanket, took our stew-bucket, and slipped silently down the foremast's rope ladder onto the deck. Tom-john sat aloft, staring at the bright moon; no one was on deck but the sleepy helmsman. Carefully I slipped down the fore stairs and threaded my way into the gloomy gunner's deck past several doors to the lesser officer's quarter's, my shrouded lantern hidden inside my coat to keep even the light glowing around its shrouds from being seen. Several gunwales stood open, letting in fresh air and a little moonlight, sailors snoring between the cannons under thick quilts. I tip-toed past and slipped unnoticed down three more flights into the deep hold. There I treaded softly, listening for any sound audible over the creaking boards, and then I slowly lifted the shrouds of my lantern. The light showed the hold empty save for the stacked cargo, Uncle Rory, and Gerome David.

"Thank God," Uncle Rory exclaimed as I handed him the bucket, and he shoveled the cold stew into his mouth with a desperation that only starvation could induce.

I examined Gerome David while Uncle Rory ate. Gerome David looked ghastly, as pale as summer clouds, and shrunken from dehydration, his skin like waterlogged parchment that had dried too fast, looking too delicate for the vindictive bully that Chad Mathew and I had grown up wrestling. Gerome David lay propped up against the hull, his lolling head wedged against a rough bulwark. I took his hand and held it up; no semblance of life showed save for the almost imperceptible rise and fall of his breathing. I brushed his hair back from his eyes; we'd grown up fighting, constantly squabbling, and taunting each other at every opportunity, but I didn't think that I could bear his loss. If Gerome David died, then I'd be his murderer; my gaff in the tavern had landed us on this floating death-trap. Even if Uncle Rory and I survived, if Gerome David died, then I'd have no family left; I could never go home and confess to Mother that my stupidity had cost her eldest son's life. I'd have to say good-bye to Uncle Rory on the shore and walk away, alone for the rest of my life.

Uncle Rory listened silently as I repeated everything that Tom-john had told me about the Pact and the capture of The Seahawk. Then we went over it all again, my every sentence interrupted by many questions. Uncle Rory asked if I'd witnessed anything to confirm animosity between Captain Beckett and Angela, or Captain Angel, as Tom-john had called her. I hadn't, but Uncle Rory smiled anyway.

"We have allies," Uncle Rory said. "At least, we've identified them."

"Allies? Only Tom-john seems friendly."

"Angela needs allies before Captain Beckett gets to the Cave of Riches."

"But the Cave of Riches is empty ...!"

"Exactly, and once they discover that, then Angela's need for us vanishes. Captain Beckett needs her men to handle this man-'o-war; he can't afford to kill Angela and her men until he gets enough money to replace them. While Angela thinks that the Cave of Riches holds her death-sentence, she'll need every hand that she can get, including you and me."

"But ... what happens when we sail into Gibbet Bay?"

"I don't know ... yet. I need time to think, to plan this out. I'm going to have to speak to Angela myself."

"I can ask her ..."

"If you tell her that you've talked to me, then we'll both be killed, and Gerome David will die without us. No; ask Angela if you can come and see me and your brother. Tell her that you're worried about us ... and that you need to talk to me. She'll ask why, and you tell her ... ummmm..., say that ... oh! Tell her how smart I am, how I taught you to read, and that I'm very book-learned. Her situation is precarious; she can't afford not to investigate a possible source of help."

For almost an hour, Uncle Rory pretended that he was Angela, and made me practice my question until I had it right. Then we poured all of the oil from my lantern into his and said good-bye.

"Remember," Uncle Rory warned, "ask Angela just like we practiced, and don't offer any more information than you have to. If you bungle again, we die."

7

THE RED PANTHEON

"A sail!" Tom-john cried. "A sail!"

I sat up, cold and confused, as the roar of boot-stomps reverberated through the ship. A cold, early dawn met the crowfoot as the waking pirates cheered and crowded to the port rail. The streaking rays of the red dawn streamed high, the eastern horizon aglow with a fiery warning of the day about to begin. Three tall sails rose above the distant, calm waters; a beautiful schooner in violent profile, waves splashing from her prow. Silhouetted against the dawn, only the rising light showed the ship; she probably hadn't spotted us yet. I smiled, delighted to wake up to such a stunning spectacle.

"To arms!" Captain Beckett cried as he stepped out from the forecastle. "Turn! Turn, you swabs!"

A chill shivered me; I'd always wanted to see a real sea pirate's waylay, but the beautiful schooner looked unexpectedly glorious, free-sailing upon the sea. Suddenly I understood Tom-john's reluctance; to sink her seemed a terrible waste. The ships that we lured into Gibbet Bay entered of their own free will, and it was God's plan that we harvested them. At least, that was what Grandpa Zachary William Wrecker had preached, and I'd heard Mother read his passage so many times that I'd never stopped to question it. I'd always admired the majesty of fine ships, and thought it sad that we had to cannibalize them. Doubtlessly these sea pirates had their own code, just like us Wreckers, and believed that God brought weaker ships within their reach for them to plunder. I didn't like that; it made the Wrecker code seem less valid. Destroying a noble ship suddenly felt wrong, and I experienced a momentary guilt, as if my whole life had been a crime.

Pirates raced up the shrouds and laid-to the lines. No one even glanced at me; they knew their business, and our ship turned so fast that we tilted hard and then rocked to the inside. I clung tight, no more afraid than on the branch of a tree back home, feeling the strong wind tousle my hair; I was a sailor at last.

"Tadpole!" Tom-john shouted. "Down! Below deck!"

"What?" I cried, offended.

"Boys should watch a fight before they join in," Tom-john said. "You'll just get in the way ..."

"I can fight!"

Several pirates laughed sarcastically while Tom-john frowned.

"Jeremy, battles are for killers."

"Give me a musket and I'll kill any man that you can see."

Their laughter died; my forceful tone surprised even me.

"Can you shoot a man in cold blood?" Tom-john asked warily.

"While he's saying his prayers," I replied.

"Can he shoot?" one of the other pirates asked doubtfully.

"Better than you," I challenged.

The other pirates laughed again as the man who'd questioned me scowled and glared, and for the first time I wasn't sure if they were laughing at me or not.

"Give him a musket," another pirate suggested. "Let him prove his boast."

Tom-john swung down to the crowfoot and looked into my eyes with alarming seriousness.

"Tadpole, are you sure?"

Ten minutes later, several sturdy muskets were passed up, handed from one pirate to the next. Tom-john hesitantly took one and handed it to me.

"Stay low," Tom-john warned. "Men who shoot from the sails are easy targets. They'll have their own men in the sheets, and aft-gunners."

"The wind's at our backs," I replied. "They'll be in our range first."

Several pirates looked impressed, casting curious glances at me. Two crowded into the crowfoot beside me and another climbed up to the foremast crown. The rest of the pirates scrambled down to the deck, but stayed near the shrouds, low behind the rail. I ignored them and looked ahead. The schooner had been sailing toward us until she spied our outline in the morning glare. As we closed, she turned away, but her maneuvers slowed her.

The Seahawk was fast for a man-'o-war, but some schooners could make fifteen knots. Captain Beckett proved masterful at maneuvering, cutting gently to one side and then the other, always slowly, never letting our speed lessen. The schooner may have been a faster ship, but it kept shifting to port, and then to starboard, each time abruptly, slowing their lead. Four hours we chased them, slowly gaining. Letters across her aft slowly came into view: The Red Pantheon. I wondered why she fled; we weren't flying pirate colors. Perhaps she wasn't sure if we were friends or enemies.

Suddenly an aft cannon blasted a fiery ball at us, but it splashed short. Then I spied large splashes beside The Red Pantheon; their sailors were tossing cargo overboard to lighten their load.

"They're stripping her," I said, and the pirate beside me paused, then stood up and shaded his eyes, staring at the schooner until another splash twinkled beside their hull.

"Youthful deadlights," he scowled, and then he turned to shout down at the deck. "Captain! They're stripping her!"

"Hold yer' stations!" Captain Beckett shouted. "Ready the fore-guns!"

Ten minutes longer we sailed, inching closer, as several more cannonballs blasted, and balls splashed ever closer.

"Fire!" Captain Beckett cried.

Mr. Roberts repeated the captain's shout, and a moment later, our long nines blasted. I watched eagerly; the only guns that I'd ever seen fired were aimed down into Gibbet Bay. Both of our ship's guns were raised high; our cannonballs arced up and fell, but neither hit. One fell short, the other splashed uselessly ten feet from their hull. But we'd made our point: they were within our range.

"Again!" Captain Beckett cried. "Fire at will!"

I clenched my musket eagerly. I'd killed over fifty men ...

Memories of the tall, proud miller's son at the village puppet show flooded over me. He'd turned around and stared at me, eyeing my Wrecker clothes in the light of the glowing sail upon which Sir Glorificus had defeated many foes: George, the boy who'd boasted of having ground over a hundred bags of flour. I remembered the shock in his eyes when I'd told him that I'd killed over fifty men. George's eyes had flown open wide, and before Uncle Rory's hand had struck the side of my head, I'd realized how strange my violent life was to boys like George. His people, folk who lived on the flatlands, didn't kill people like Wreckers and pirates. They lived peaceful lives where their twin brothers didn't die during waylays.

I shook my head and forced the weak thought away. I had another brother, below deck, who might die if I didn't prove myself now. For Gerome David, I steeled myself; I had to be a Wrecker.

Their cannon-fire hit us first. One cannonball arced low and clipped the starboard bowsprit yard, bounced across the main deck, and smashed through the wall below the poop deck. Lucky pirates jumped away from it too late to matter; had they been caught in its path, then they would've died. Our next volley struck The Red Pantheon square through its trumpeter's cabin, and another swept just inside their rail; it couldn't have damaged their ship much, but two sailors fell overboard, and neither ship stopped to rescue them. Their cannons returned fire and ours blasted constantly. Our whole ship shook as our fore-hull took a cannonball hard, and I glanced at the sailors beside me, worried, then looked up to see Tom-john, riding the tall main mast cap, waving his hat like a madman and calling for them to aim at him. I grimaced: *I wasn't going to lose Tom-john!* I cocked my hammer and sighted down the barrel.

"Too far, boy," the pirate beside me said. "Another minute or two before they're in range."

I grinned without looking at him. I'd grown up shooting; I took careful aim.

"Middle man on the poop-rail," I said.

I squeezed my trigger. The familiar explosion blasted in my right ear, and then the very man that I'd signified toppled out of sight.

"Bluebeard's coffin!" the pirate exclaimed, and he raised his rifle and fired.

I never saw if he hit anything or not, busy reloading my weapon, but a dozen rifles suddenly fired from both ships. Shot hit the sail above me, but I ignored it; in a waylay, only the next round was important. I rammed in another ball and raised my musket, the pirate beside me still pouring his powder.

"Tadpole's a marksman," he said to the pirate beside him.

I aimed and fired again. My second shot missed; The Red Pantheon's men were now ducked below the poop rail, firing between the slots. I reloaded, then spied a muzzle-flash from their mizzen-top. I aimed carefully, then flinched as the pirate jostled me to raise his own musket.

"Mizzen-top," I said.

Again I fired true, and this time the pirates below cheered as a body toppled from their mizzen-top and crashed onto their poop.

"You can shoot alongside me anytime," the pirate beside me said.

The constant roar of cannons and muskets grew louder as we closed range. The pirate in the forepeak above us cried out and fell past us, down to the deck with a meaty thud, his musket broken beneath him. A cannonball flew at us and struck the fore-mast inches over our heads, making all of us duck as splinters showered into our hair. I glanced up; a raw gash as deep as my fist and a handswidth tall was gouged from the foremast, which trembled and vibrated alarmingly. All three of us on the crowfoot glanced worriedly at each other, and then we raised our muskets and fired as one.

Their rear hull shattered with a resounding crash-clang; we'd hit one of their cannons with a cannonball. We were so close that we could hear their panicked cries and shouts of dismay. Then, abruptly, they stopped shooting, and a loud whistle sounded.

"This is it!" the pirate beside me cried.

Slowly a white flag slid up The Red Pantheon's mizzen-mast. We'd done it; The Red Pantheon was surrendering.

"Cease fire!" Mr. Roberts bellowed. "Grappling hooks! Stand ready at the port guns!"

"Reload," the pirate beside me instructed as I lowered my musket. "They could be luring us in."

I quickly reloaded, but it wasn't necessary. Sailors jumped into their rigging; their sails were quickly raised, and pirates jumped to our shrouds, heading to our yards. I started to follow, eager to help, but the pirate beside me grabbed my shoulder and held me down.

"They go," he said grimly. "We protect them."

Captain Beckett slid us beside the old schooner's starboard side, close enough that we could see our opponents. Disgust twisted our defeated opponent's stern expressions, matched only by shame and disappointment. I stared down my barrel, ready, but their dropped weapons lay on their deck. I'd never seen such misery; victims of Wrecker waylays never faced a long defeat. Grappling hooks were tossed, hooked onto sturdy rails, and reined in from both sides, pulling the ships together. Their captain, a tall, well-built man in a high-plumed hat, white wig, and a bright red outfit liberally trimmed with gold, stood before all of his men, stiff and stoic, resigned to die nobly. A gangplank reached out from The Red Pantheon to The Seahawk and was quickly secured. Pirates rushed across, wielding pistols and cutlasses, but not one of their men moved. Captain Beckett strode across alone, our pirates clearing his path. Every eye above deck watched him.

Their captain faced ours without flinching. Slowly he drew his sword and held it out. Captain Beckett took it from him.

"Captain Cornelius Godsworth, at your service," their captain said.

"Captain Beckett," ours concluded the introduction. "The Red Pantheon and all lives on it are mine."

"Sir, by the articles of the sea, I beg quarter for my men."

Captain Beckett glared about the deck, then up at the furled sails.

"A fine ship; be a shame to sink her," Captain Beckett said.

"Your terms, sir?"

Captain Beckett paused. Footsteps sounded on the gangplank and he turned around; Angela strode across to their ship, walked right up to Captain Beckett, and met his stare.

"As I said, a shame to sink such a fine ship," Captain Beckett said, and then he turned back to Captain Godsworth. "What's in your hold?"

"Passengers are the bulk of our cargo," Captain Godsworth replied. "We have large stores of salted beef and eight cannons meant for Fort Cadaveral, two-hundred pounders, and several dozen kegs of powder. We also are conveying six fine carriages for Master-General Fortescue."

"Show me your passengers."

At least twenty men in elaborate court finery were forced on deck and paraded before Captain Beckett. Six women cowered behind them, three of them very old and obviously frightened. Captain Beckett stepped forward to examine the terrified women, paused before one pretty young woman, but he passed by them all without comment. I stared amazed; not once in my life had a ship carrying women sailed into Gibbet Bay.

Captain Beckett turned to face Captain Godsworth.

"What would you give me for safe passage for your ship?" Captain Beckett asked.

Captain Godsworth looked stunned, and eyes widened on every face on both crews.

"No!" Angela cried angrily. "I need a ship!"

"You'll take what yer captain gives you, like it or not!" Captain Beckett shouted at Angela.

Angela fumed, and then suddenly she turned and stormed back across the gangplank, her boots shaking its thin wooden planks, and she immediately stomped down the stairs, vanishing below deck. Every eye watched her go. Once she'd vanished, Captain Beckett turned back to Captain Godsworth.

"Most honorable Captain Beckett, name your price."

"All of your silver, gold, and copper," Captain Beckett said loudly, so everyone could hear. "Every coin, every piece of jewelry, every gem: everything of any value. Withhold one coin, one trinket, and I'll sink your ship with all hands. All of your weapons and powder, too. Toss your big guns overboard; I can't use them and don't want any fort to have them. And half of your pork. And I want fifteen of your men, good sailors, willing to publically swear to me. You can choose which; former pirates are best. Do that, and swear to me that not a farthing or pistol remains on your ship, and you can keep her. Oh, and all of your rum; my men are thirsty."

A loud cheer rose from Captain Beckett's crew, but a few remained silent, all of whom I recognized as

Angela's old crew; the more men that joined Captain Beckett's crew the closer they were to a second betrayal. I looked up at Tom-john, but he was clinging high on the main mast, waving a large white gull-feather at The Red Pantheon, admiring her sails and rigging, seeming oblivious to what everyone else was intently watching.

An hour later, with both crews working diligently, the rape of The Red Pantheon was complete. Women stood without rings, necklaces, or bracelets, sailors without their earrings, and two small chests of wealth sat on the deck beside Captain Beckett's boots. Our deck was crowded with pork, weapons, and plunder like our sheds back home, and pirates were hoisting net-loads of powder-barrels through the main hold-doors into our hull. Every one of our pirates had a new musket, pistol, or cutlass; the belts of the sailors aboard The Red Pantheon hung slack and empty around their waists. Fifteen sailors stood before Captain Beckett and swore to be pirates under his command, and Captain Godsworth was forced to bear witness, and then declare all of them outlaws. Mr. Roberts had the two treasure chests transferred by the fifteen new recruits under his close supervision, and Captain Beckett returned Captain Godsworth's sword, then marched across the gangplank, leaving that one captain's saber as their only weapon. The last of our men followed and the gangplank was withdrawn. Lines were released; our ships parted, and Captain Beckett bellowed.

"Stand down the guns! Set sail!"

We sailed away, leaving The Red Pantheon stripped but intact. They set sail moments after us, and turned opposite to our heading at first breeze. Twenty minutes later, The Red Pantheon's sails were only a white puff on the horizon.

Tom-john sidled down beside me.

"Lad, your musket-balls were blessed by God," Tom-john said reverently. "I thought my deadlights were deceiving me; you're a true killer."

I smiled, but then I grimly turned away. I couldn't tell anyone, not even Tom-john, where and how I'd learned to shoot, or the secret shame of my feelings of regret. At least Captain Beckett hadn't sunk The Red Pantheon; the proud ship had survived. Tom-john stuck another feather into my hair.

"Tadpole True-shot," Tom-john grinned. "That's your name now. God has touched you."

I grinned weakly, then looked down.

"Captain Angel wasn't pleased," I said.

"Aye, in a right fury," Tom-john agreed, shaking his head sadly. "I'd have been happy to fly on those schooner-masts, even if they were shorter than these."

"Tadpole!" Mr. Roberts shouted up from the deck.

Tom-john and I glanced down. Evening had fallen, but the deck was crowded with pirates. Captain Beckett had ordered a barrel of rum to be opened and served out to the whole crew, and many were already drunk, laughing and prancing about amid several piping flutes and a poorly-played accordion. We'd been relaxing in the crowfoot, sharing a bottle of rum, when Mr. Roberts' cry startled us.

"Now, Tadpole! Captain Beckett wants ya."

"Best hurry, lad," Tom-john whispered.

Seconds later, my feet hit the deck, and Mr. Roberts led me into the captain's quarters. I tried to quell my nervousness; I'd been in plenty of captain's quarters, although always swimming. This captain's cabin was no different, save that it was much larger. It had the same ornate table, chairs, and maps on its walls, wide windows, and worthless clutter, save for the two chests that had been pirated from Captain Godsworth's schooner. Captain Beckett, Angela, and two other pirates sat at the table, finishing dinner, still sipping wine. Mr. Roberts stepped past me and sat in the only unoccupied chair; every eye was upon me.

"Tadpole, I hear that you shoot well," Captain Beckett said.

"Yes, sir."

"I hear you're a very good shot, that you plucked off an officer when my other marksmen thought that we were out of range, and that you seldom missed any target."

I nodded.

"I could use a good shot on my crew. I pay very well and our prospects are excellent; we're the only pirates in these waters with a man-'o-war."

I stood frozen, worried; if I refused, would Captain Beckett kill me? If I died, what chance would Uncle Rory have? Uncle Rory might be able to escape at night, but Gerome David would certainly die. Yet, if I accepted, would I ever be able to escape?

"Yes," I said.

"Excellent!" Captain Beckett smiled. "We'll set up a berth ..."

"I'd like to stay with Tom-john ... in the sheets," I interjected.

Captain Beckett fired a dark glance at Angela, who looked surprised. Mr. Roberts narrowed his eyes suspiciously.

"In the sheets?" Captain Beckett asked. "There're warmer berths ..."

"Tom-john's my friend," I said, but I didn't like their silent glares, so I added. "He ... doesn't frighten me."

Captain Beckett burst out laughing.

"Madmen don't frighten you, but my crew does," Captain Beckett said between hearty guffaws. "Tadpole, you delight me. Honest and a light heart; you'll make a good pirate ... once you're toughened up. Welcome to my crew. Anything you need, see Mr. Roberts. Until then, climb back to your roost and tell Tom-john that my offer stands for him, too."

"Yes, sir," I said, and I awkwardly bowed and exited while Captain Beckett continued to laugh. Several other voices laughed with him, but no feminine voice joined them. I frowned; this complicated everything.

"Well?" Tom-john asked as I ascended.

"He asked me to join his crew," I said.

"Did you?"

"I said yes; I was afraid to say anything else."

Tom-john sighed and shook his head.

"He said that his offer stood for you, too."

"Aye, any captain would," Tom-john said softly. "He can't kill Angela while all of her men remain loyal, but if he could draw us away ..."

"I ... I'd rather ... have Angel ... as my captain," I whispered hesitantly.

Tom-john' eyes widened, and then he smiled wanly. He reached up and pulled a gray gull feather from his cap, solemnly touched it to both my ears and nose, and then handed it to me with great reverence. Then he leaned forward and kissed my forehead, put one finger to his lips, and shushed me.

"Tell no one. Go up."

He handed his lit lantern to me and pointed upwards. I scaled the main mast high, but Tom-john didn't follow; he slipped over onto the starboard shrouds and clung there, silent and not moving. Soon I sat in the top armour, worried that I'd done something wrong. A slow hour passed before he moved.

The door to the captain's quarters finally opened. Mr. Roberts came out, followed by the two other pirates, and lastly came Angela. Each headed to their separate destinations, Mr. Roberts to the first officer's cabin, the two men below deck, and Angela to one of the lesser officer's cabins. Tom-john slipped down as soon as all had vanished, crept along the rail to Angela's door, swept off his hat and softly knocked. A moment later, her door opened and, to my surprise, Tom-john whispered something to Angela, and she pulled him inside and closed her door.

I sat on the main mast wondering what I should do. Should I sneak back down to Uncle Rory? What was Tom-john doing? Another hour passed, and then Angela's door opened, but no light showed from within. Two figures slipped out, crept to the shrouds, and climbed with practiced ease.

"Douse your lantern!" Angela whispered urgently.

I blew out the flame, and then Angela and Tom-john joined me on the top armour. Angela looked threatening as always, one muscled, tattooed arm reaching over me to cling to a mast line, her strong jaw set as she faced me, her stare closer than ever. I hadn't realized how beautiful she was; perhaps the pale starlight softened her, or the fact that she was wearing only a brown leather vest and a half-skirt, free of the many weapons that she always wore.

"Tom-john says that you wish to swear to someone other than Captain Beckett," Angela said.

"M-meaning n-no offense," I stammered, trying not to stare into the deep shadow of her bulging cleavage. "I just ... well, he frightens me."

Angela scowled and started to turn away.

"Please, mistress," Tom-john said.

Angela paused, then faced me again.

"You swore to Captain Beckett ..."

"I-I was afraid that he'd kill me ... and not just for m-myself, begging your pardon."

"But you don't like Captain Beckett?"

"He threw my brother and uncle into the hull. I haven't seen them since we were brought here. I'm ... afraid for them."

"This Cave of Riches we're following; is it real?"

"Yes, ... at least, I assume so. I hope so."

"So you have seen it before!"

"No, ma'm, I swear! It's just ... if it's not real ...!"

"Captain Beckett will keel-haul you if there's no treasure," Angela finished. "So, what do you want?"

"I want to see my uncle ... and my brother. My uncle's very smart, book-learned; he taught me how to read ... and knows everything."

"Why do you want to see him?"

"Be-because ... he'll tell me what to do. I'm sure to do wrong without him. He's so smart ...!"

Angela considered in silence, eyeing me warily.

"I need to know that they're alright," I said. "I'll do anything ... *anything!* ... to help them."

Angela and Tom-john exchanged glances.

"Has anyone been taking care of the prisoners?" Angela asked.

"I haven't been below since we took The Seahawk," Tom-john answered.

Angela frowned.

"I'll see to it, at least; see that they get food and water. Book-learned, you say? Tell me, Tadpole; you're sworn to Captain Beckett now, but if I see that your relatives are cared for, would you use your ... impressive marksmanship ... for me?"

"Of course."

"No matter who I tell you to shoot?"

"Any target; just ... please, help my brother and uncle."

"You do understand ... if you breathe one word of this ..."

"No, never; I swear!"

Angela stared at me until I cringed; her glare stabbed like frozen knives. Then she reached up to Tom-john's hat, pulled free one of his long feathers, and handed it to me.

"Thank you, Captain Angel," I said.

"My Angel," Tom-john said, and to my amazement, Angela extended her hand. Gently Tom-john took her hand and tenderly he kissed it. I stared in disbelief as she smiled at him.

Without a word or a sound, Angela slid back down the shrouds and vanished into the deck's shadows.

Jay Palmer

8

THE SECOND MARKER

I hadn't ruined everything. I hadn't worded my question to Angela exactly as Uncle Rory had specified, but I'd gotten his intention across. *Would Angela help Uncle Rory? Even with Angela's help, would Gerome David survive?*

Captain Beckett's pirates crowded the deck. The sun was bright and glaring, but cool breezes kept the day from getting too hot, and a sweet scent filled the air, a perfume of the sea, like flowers in spring, which was unusual this late in the year. I inhaled deeply, reveling in the air's cleanliness filling my lungs. Back home, on a day like today, I'd be romping across the cliffs overlooking Gibbet Bay with Margaret Blythe, Kevin John, Devin Elliot, and all my other cousins, searching for hidden treasure-caves, laughing and playing. I missed them all, which was ironic; all the while that I'd been playing with them, I'd dreamed of having exciting adventures sailing the sea with real pirates. Wreckers were pirates, but we were also family. Grandpa Jack, in his slow, monotonous way, commanded loyalty far more than Captain Beckett. Grandpa Barnaby must've understood that; he'd tried to explain it, but I hadn't understood. Loyalty is easily voiced, but proven only in actions.

The pirates were more-friendly to me today; my marksmanship under enemy fire had earned their respect, but I felt only scorn for them. Gone were their black looks and derisive sneers, replaced by nods of approval and occasional brown-toothed smiles, but they'd turn against me just as easily. One pirate offered me a drink from his cup of grog, which I gladly accepted, and he invited me to join them in the galley after dark; I suspected that Captain Beckett had told them to buddy up to me after I'd swore to join his crew.

I was getting more accustomed to life in the sheets; the sway of the masts now pleased me, like I was playfully rocking back and forth on the top branches of a tall, strong tree. Tom-john had taught me the complex order of the lines and pulleys, the web of ropes that held ships together and flexed with the sway, which reinforced its structure and reassured me that I wasn't going to fall. Standing on the flat deck was nowhere near as fun as clinging to shrouds, perching on the top armour, or climbing to the cap and feeling like a bird flying free in the wind. The coarse tautness of the ropes and the smooth feel of the varnished masts reassured my hands.

I glanced upwards from my perch on the crowfoot, seeing the repaired mast. The ship's carpenter had carefully measured the ruin of the cannonball that had almost taken my head off, and then brought up a segment of wood, a jar of glue, and a box of tools. The wood had been purposefully cut too large. He sawed out the shattered section of mast, shaved his segment of wood until it fit perfectly, and then he firmly glued it in place. After wrapping it tightly in a long length of gray cord, he ordered me to leave it be until it dried, and said that he'd come back then to clean and finish the surface properly. The foremast looked like it was bandaged with a swollen lump, and I was determined to watch when the carpenter removed its wrappings, shaped, cleaned, and re-shellacked his masterful repair.

Tom-john was out on the repaired bowsprit, leaning over the water-splashing prow. He seemed to be playing like a child, oblivious to his dangerous perch. Captain Beckett's crew on deck far below seemed eager, and I looked up to see a dark shimmer on the North horizon.

"L-l-land h-ho!" I shouted hesitantly, and every eye turned up to me.

"You sure?" Mr. Roberts shouted up from the deck.

"Aye," I shouted back.

Minutes later, Captain Beckett strode out onto deck. We were closer now; even the men on deck could see the rising dark shelf, and Tom-john scrambled up beside me, patted my shoulder, and grinned idiotically.

"What?" I asked.

"Your treasure map," Tom-john said, looking incredulously at me. "You really didn't look at it, did you?"

"The second marker!" I gasped, amazed. These cliffs had to be it, the location of the latitudinal coordinate, carved by Grandpa Zachary Wrecker almost a century ago. I stood up on the spar and looked out; I'd pictured those three clefts in the cliff that marked our exact destination since I was five; I was about to finally see them.

We sailed over an hour right toward the cliffs, which grew taller as we approached, until they towered over our masts. Three rugged, jagged clefts in the rock stood darkly upon the cliff-face. Mr. Roberts bellowed the expected orders and the pirates jumped to shorten the sails as we steered toward them.

"Weigh anchor!" Captain Beckett shouted. "Lower a gunboat!"

Pirates scrambled to obey.

"Permission to lead the boat," Angela asked loudly.

Captain Beckett turned and stared at her. Angela stood as I'd first seen her, heavily-armed, bared tattoos bright in the sunlight against her sun-bronzed skin, her long, dark hair blowing in the wind. Captain Beckett eyed her, examined the cliff again, and then nodded.

"Tadpole!" Angela cried.

I hesitated, then almost leaped down the rigging. I grabbed a runner, swung, and landed on the shrouds with ease. Many pirates laughed.

"Tadpole's a baby Tom-john!"

I couldn't hold back my grin.

My feet hit the deck and I helped push the gunboat over the edge, then stood eagerly as they winched it down. A rope Jacob's ladder was dropped over the edge, and soon I was climbing down, against the wide hull, into the tiny boat. The only difference in this crew was that these men carried muskets and pistols; I hoped that they wouldn't be used, since I was the only one unarmed. But I couldn't believe my luck; I'd seen the first marker, and now I was going to see the second. Even Grandpa Barnaby hadn't seen both.

Angela climbed down last, settling herself in the fore just as the hooks were released and hauled up by our shipmates. I sat in the rear as the oarsmen pulled hard. One wave crashed against the great ship's hull and sprayed all of us, but soon we were rowing away toward the left-most cleft.

When we reached the cleft, Angela stood first, and several pirates tried to join her.

"Stay in the boat," Angela ordered them. "Tadpole, you're with me."

Several groaned in complaint, but Angela viscously seized the closest, silently threatening him with her furious glare, and he relented. As they turned to glare at me, I realized that these were all pirates loyal to Captain Beckett; Angela's command was precarious.

I climbed past the rowers and followed Angela. With the ease of scaling a shroud, Angela snaked up inside the biggest rough, rocky cleft. I followed, more used to climbing cliffs than she, but these rocks were wind-smoothed, their handholds slippery and uncertain. As we rose, birds flew about us by the dozens, loud-squawking gulls, crows, and many finches. Finally we spied it; a tiny cave, no more than four feet deep, filled with old, dried bird's nests. On the back wall, clearly inscribed in the stone, but too small to be read from a distance, lay the final coordinate.

"Fifty-one degrees, eight minutes north," I read.

"I can read," Angela said. "I brought you here to talk: I've spoken to your Uncle Rory. He's willing to help. He said that you're to do as I say, no matter what."

I nodded.

"I've sent Slim, one of my men, to care for your brother, too; Slim says that he'll live. Are you still ready to shoot for me?"

"Yes."

"Your target is Captain Beckett."

I paled and swallowed hard.

"Don't shoot until I say."

"They took my musket."

"I'll get you one, but not until right beforehand."

"When?"

"Soon."

"Why not wait?"

"Why wait?"

I nodded toward the pirates waiting for us below.

"Once you have the Golden Twinkle, they'll have more reason to follow you."

"Golden Twinkle ...?"

"That's ... what my brother calls it: the gleam of hidden treasure. I mean, until you have it, why should Captain Beckett's men follow you ... and not Mr. Roberts?"

Angela appraised me for a moment.

"You're smart, Tadpole," she said appreciatively. "We've been here too long; say nothing about this."

The squawking birds taunted us as we descended to the gunboat and rowed back. Minutes later, we ascended the ladder and climbed over the rail.

"We have it," Angela said, and the deck-full of pirates cheered.

"What took so long?" Captain Beckett demanded.

"The numbers were faint, almost washed away," Angela lied. "We had to read them by feel."

Captain Beckett glared at Angela, then spoke softly. "Well?"

"Fifty-one degrees, eight minutes north," Angela said.

"Mr. Roberts, as soon as the gunboat's secured, set sail ...," Captain Beckett said, "... *for my treasure.*"

The pirates cheered again, all but Angela's men. I jumped to and climbed the lower shrouds; Tom-john was at the pendant throwing breadcrumbs to a dozen squawking gulls. He looked oblivious as always, but was he really? He seemed mad, but was it a pretense?

Everyone jumped to when the order came, and I helped spread four sheets. Quickly our sails fully opened, billowed by the wind. The breeze pushed us away from the second marker with an old, sweet fragrance that I'd never smelled aboard The Seahawk: the scent of home; we were sailing toward Gibbet Bay.

Few stars shone through the many clouds that night. Gibbet Bay was days away, but I couldn't wait to get back, to rejoin my family. I had to talk to Uncle Rory, to tell him that I'd talked to Angela again. Long after dark, I silently slipped down the shrouds, after pretending to fall asleep, reached the shadowy deck, and crept down the narrow, creaking stairs, my eyes straining to see through the utter darkness below deck.

A raspy voice spoke suddenly, making me startle.

"Tadpole? That you?"

I froze; one of Captain Beckett's pirates, a tall, thin, grizzled old man with a ragged scarf holding back his matted gray hair, stepped toward me into a thin beam of light from a lonely port.

"So, tired of wind and chaffing? Good boy; the galley's this way."

His hand touched my arm and directed me, and I heard sarcastic laughter from farther back in the darkness; this pirate wasn't alone. Caught, I walked as directed, and stumbled around the iron guns before the opened middle tyre ports, through which only dim starlight was shining. I tripped on something unseen but caught myself; I couldn't appear nervous. I'd been invited down here and Captain Beckett had told his pirates to be friendly to me, but I couldn't help feeling I was being led to my doom.

Light flared in the galley. Lanterns gently swung back and forth from chains on the galley ceiling as the ship slowly rocked. The narrow tables were full of Captain Beckett's pirates and many from The Red Pantheon. Harsh voices spoke softly, like in the seedy port tavern where I'd gotten drunk and ruined everything. I had to remember that; I couldn't hold my rum.

"Look who's joined us!" the grizzled pirate behind me cried, and every eye lifted to spy me. A few voices cheered, but the room was too full, the corners in deep shifting shadows, to discern who'd welcomed me.

"Well, little Tom-john!" sneered a short, gruff sailor with greasy brown hair who looked as if he'd never bathed, but whose knotted muscles kept anyone from mentioning it.

"A pleasure," I said, nodding to him. Many laughed.

"Tadpole, this is Slicer," the pirate who'd led me said. "I'm Pete, and that's Pistol, Chuckie, Bard, and Hardback. We're Captain Beckett's oldest crewmates."

Each nodded or lifted their ale in salute except Slicer, who glared in stony silence. Pistol was short and thin, wearing a ragged shirt and a red bandana. Chuckie had a bright grin with only a few missing teeth, was bald as a cannonball, and wore a leather jerkin and breeches. A grim, dark-skinned man, Bard stared at me, his white eyes brightly shining in the lantern light; Bard said nothing, merely nodded with a deep frown, acknowledging me only enough to obey orders. Sitting at a table, nursing a tall cup, Hardback was an older man, but huge and thickly-muscled, the kind of pirate whose very presence intimidated, but he smiled at me warmly.

"A rum for Tadpole, our newest shipmate!" Chuckie cried.

"Tadpole True-shot," said a familiar voice, and I spied the pirate who'd crouched beside me in the crowfoot during the schooner-waylay. He rose from the back and came forward, sliding between the men. A wooden cup of rum passed across the room hand-to-hand; he took it and brought it to me. "Respects, men; Tadpole may not be much of a sailor, but I've never seen a better shot. He made Captain Godsworth fear us."

"Aye, he can shoot," Slicer scowled, "but can he drink?"

I hesitated, holding the rum in my hand; I couldn't get drunk, but I feared getting beaten if I refused. I'd been drinking scavenged rum all my life, and had even tasted Grandpa Jack Benjamin's special brew a few times, although it always burned my throat and stole my voice for hours. I took a deep breath and drank the rum-cup empty in one gulp. Many pirates cheered, and nodding heads bobbed all around.

"A true sea-dog ain't just a lubber who's sworn an oath," Bard scowled. "Every hand must be counted on to support the majority."

I stared, afraid to reply. Many pirates stared eagerly at me, grinning, while others exchanged doubtful looks. I could feel their eagerness tighten in my throat with the finality of a noose-necktie, but I forced myself to remain calm, not to over-react.

"Do you support the majority?" I asked.

Bard jumped to his feet, reaching for the black sheath in his belt, but as he drew its blade, hands from all around seized him and held him back.

"Beckett!" one man said warningly as Pete's hand closed on my shoulder and pulled me back, away from Bard's glaring fury.

Bard shrugged hard, throwing off the many grips. His glare never left me, but he sheathed his dagger and reached for his rum, emptied his cup in one gulp, and then stormed out through another door. Several pirates stared about uneasily.

"There's a lot of empty berths in the hold, if you're willing," Hardback spoke up. "You don't have to sleep in the wind and cold."

"Aye, Tom-john's too crazy to be a good sailor," someone said. "You should stay down here."

"Thanks, ... no," I said.

"Why not?" Slicer demanded. "Why stay aloft with Tom-john?"

I stared at all of the pirates, swallowed hard, and stammered.

"T-T-Tom-john doesn't s-s-scare me."

All the pirates burst into laughter. I feigned a smile; these pirates liked evoking fear; I'd just complimented them all.

"Tom-john's teaching me to handle the rigging," I added. "Good ... pirates ... should know that."

"Bucko," Pete said. "Make room for Tadpole; let him sit among us."

I fumbled a few words of reluctance, but no one heeded me. I was pushed to sit beside Slicer, across from Hardback.

"Drink up, boy," Chuckie said. "Another rum for Tadpole!"

"One rum per sailor," someone complained.

"Nonsense; this is Tadpole's first night, and we need to make him *welcome*," Chuckie said, placing a great emphasis on the word, as if reminding them of their orders. Some of the pirates grumbled darkly, but another rum was passed over and placed before me. I'd quickly finished my first rum, trying not to insult anyone, and closed my hand nervously around the second cup.

"So, Tadpole, where you from?" someone asked.

I never saw who asked, so I spoke to everyone.

"My ... Uncle Rory's farm," I said, and several faces soured, "but I always dreamed of sailing. I even know a few pirate songs."

This pronouncement enlivened everyone, and several called for a song. I grinned; Grandpa Barnaby had taught us many lively songs, and I picked an old favorite. By the time that I was half-finished with the first stanza, half of the crew was singing, and I sang louder.

Only man-jacks sail the Barbary coast
From skysail to spanker raise the toast
No cabotage sailors of fortune host
Only man-jacks sail the Barbary coast
   A lubber's line leads none astray
   The helm held tight toward the headway
   Man the gunwales and slipway
   With the wind, the anchor aweigh
Only man-jacks sail the Barbary coast
From skysail to spanker raise the toast
No cabotage sailors of fortune host
Only man-jacks sail the Barbary coast
   Keel-haul the snotty, the lagan back
   Jurymast the boatswain if there's a lack
   Ride the jibboom larboard to tack
   Every true salt sails under one ship's jack
Only man-jacks sail the Barbary coast
From skysail to spanker raise the toast
No cabotage sailors of fortune host

Only man-jacks sail the Barbary coast

All evening we sang songs and drank, and I was feeling giddy ere we finished, my head spinning from the powerful rum. I'd always dreamed of singing in a galley full of real pirates, and I was starting to wonder if I wouldn't enjoy this life; sailing and attacking ships with no Grandpa Jack or Great Aunt Pearl ordering me to do chores. But the memory of my lost twin held my mirth in check; Gerome David was half-dead; fully-dead, if I ruined our chances again. I pretended to need to pee and escaped as everyone was laughing after the crew finished singing *M' hearty ale.* I quickly slipped out of the galley, almost forgotten by the revelers as the slow drone of *Poor Eric's necktie* began. I hurried to the stairs, glanced about into the blackness for the gleam of watching eyes, and then fled down the narrow, unseen steps, determined to see Uncle Rory before dawn.

As I reached the bottom, I regretted not trying to steal a lantern; total darkness removed my sight. I suspected that none of the pirates were down here, but I couldn't be certain. I reached out and felt a wooden crate beside the door; how was I to navigate my way to Uncle Rory?

"Wrecker," I whispered, my voice hissing over the creaking hull and the squeak of a mouse.

"Jeremy?" Uncle Rory's voice called.

"I've no light."

"Wait there."

A moment later, footsteps creaked toward me.

"Where are you?"

"Here."

Familiar fingers touched.

"Where are we now?"

"Are we alone?" I asked.

"Yes."

"We're sailing home."

"They found the second marker."

"Yes; Angela and I found it."

"Captain Angel? That's bad."

"Why?"

"Captain Beckett's looking for an excuse to kill Angela, don't you see? He's giving her all of the rope that he can, hoping that she'll hang herself. Her men's solidarity won't survive if she doesn't, but he daren't kill her outright, not without starting a mutiny."

"Angela wants me to kill Captain Beckett."

"When?"

"She hasn't told me yet."

"Soon, I'll warrant. I heard about your shooting during the waylay; Captain Beckett's changed his opinion about you."

"He made me swear to him."

"Good. Now, don't take that oath too seriously; you're a Wrecker first, and if we fail, then our whole family dies."

"What are we going to do?"

"Escape, of course, but not until the last minute."

"How?"

"We blow The Seahawk."

"What ...? How ...?"

"Leave that to me. I haven't been just sitting here; since you found me, I've explored most of the ship while everyone's asleep. We've still got two days before we get home; I'll fuse the powder room and stand ready to light it. As soon as the family starts the waylay, I'll light the fuse and carry Gerome David to the deck. We bail over the side aft, by the keel; that'll be the safest place when the powder ignites."

"What about our friends?"

"Friends ...?"

"Tom-john, Angela, and her men ..."

"I'll warn our friends. You mind yourself; as we sail into Gibbet Bay, don't expose yourself; Margaret Blythe won't wait to identify brothers or uncle before she squeezes her trigger, and I don't want her bragging about having killed you. Once the ship blows, swim for the Cave of Riches; we'll be safe enough in there until they recognize our voices."

"How will we all get inside ...?"

"Mind what I say, nothing else!" Uncle Rory shook me hard, warningly. "You listen, do exactly as I say, and don't stop for anything. I might get shot, and Gerome David ... even if we get killed, you get inside the cave as fast as you can. Don't wait for anyone or anything; we won't wait for you. Do you understand?"

"Yes, Uncle."

"Remember, we're not safe until Captain Beckett and all of his men are dead, so from now on don't talk to anybody, if you can help it. Say nothing, not even to Tom-john or Angela. Pretend that you know nothing. Our lives, yours, your brother's, and mine, ... and all our friends ... have one chance to survive and not murder our whole clan; you ruined our chances before, and if you ruin everything again then I'll kill you myself."

Jay Palmer

9

ANGELA'S PIRATES

The next day was cloudy, cold, and chill; few pirates came above deck, and those that did wore thick coats and quickly vanished below. Twice Captain Beckett and Angela appeared beside the helm, but they soon returned indoors. Mr. Robert's voice occasionally wafted up; shouts at the men to work harder. I wondered what chores they were doing, but I didn't dare investigate.

I shivered inside my bulky coat; the wind blew strong, seeping inside my coat to steal my warmth. Tom-john spent the morning swinging all over the high rigging; a seagull had landed on one of the yards and Tom-john kept trying to attract it with food, but every time that he got close, the seagull flapped away to rest on another yard.

Around noon, a great clamor startled me. Cries burst from below, and soon the deck swarmed with angry pirates. Mr. Roberts charged out, shouting at all of them, but not until Captain Beckett appeared did silence fall. I sat on the lower main yard, watching, and Tom-john slid down beside me, his face anxious, his seagull forgotten.

"What is it?" I asked.

"Oh, no," Tom-john said unhappily, deep concern in his voice. "It's Keeler; *not again!*"

"Who's Keeler?"

"One of our mates."

A large, brown-coated man was hauled forward and forced to kneel before Captain Beckett. Many hands gripped him tightly. He struggled, but not much, as if resigned.

"We heard him!" Slicer shouted. "He said that he'd never swear to Captain Beckett!"

Tom-john winced as many angry voices growled in agreement. Angela stepped forward and slapped Keeler's face so hard that the smack resounded.

"Swear to Captain Beckett!" Angela shouted at him.

Keeler's head rocked backwards, and then his reluctant voice rang out.

"I swear ... to Captain Beckett!"

Many scowled, and some softly cursed.

"Will that do?" I asked Tom-john.

Tom-john shook his head.

"What good has your oath ever been?" Captain Beckett finally said, and many pirates grunted approvingly. "You're worse than Breakwater. Keel-haul him."

The pirates cheered. Suddenly Keeler started struggling hard, but many hands seized and lifted him.

"Stop fighting!" Tom-john hissed, although only I could hear him. Keeler uselessly struggled against the captain's order.

"Cat!" Captain Beckett shouted angrily.

The pirates cheered again. A fury of pushing and shoving followed. Keeler flailed and twisted, but many hands tore his huge brown coat from him and dragged him to a cannon, laid him face down over it, and Keeler's hands and feet were quickly bound fast around the heavy iron gun.

"Can't we do anything?" I asked Tom-john.

"Not without making it worse," Tom-john said. "Speaking against the captain's a prime offense; even Captain Angel once had to punish Keeler."

"Why?"

"He can't keep his mouth shut," Tom-john replied. "He's done this before, the ass. Once he was keel-hauled twice; angry after one keel-hauling, he cursed Captain Silver-tooth, and got a second keel-hauling right afterwards. He took months to heal; we were amazed that he survived."

Grinning wickedly, the pirates drew back from Keeler's bound form. Keeler had stopped struggling. Angela stepped forward.

"Open his shirt," Angela said.

One pirate came forward with a drawn dagger, sliced Keeler's thin, ragged shirt clean up the middle, from shirt-tail to collar, and laid it aside. Keeler's heavily-scarred skin looked like a patchwork-quilt; long cords of rippled scars crisscrossed his muscular back. Angela pulled the cat from her belt and then slashed the air before her with a loud swish, audible even over the rushing wind. I winced; I'd scavenged several cat-o-nine-tail's from waylaid ships. A cat was a leather-wrapped handle with nine tri-braided rawhide laces, three feet from handle-top to its knotted-tips. A cat could flay skin from bone with a single lash; not a deadly weapon: cats were designed to induce pain.

I stared down upon the anxious scene; the tensions of the crew were growing, and this wouldn't cool anyone's mood. Holding the cat, Angela looked stern and dangerous, but she was still a woman. *How could she ...?*

Whack!

I flinched almost as badly as Keeler, who failed to stifle his pained moan. My foot slipped from the yard; only Tom-john's strong grip saved me from falling. A few pirates cheered, but most winced as Tom-john had. Almost everyone looked sad.

Whack!

Keeler cried out. Red lines appeared on his back.
Whack!

I turned away, unable to look, but Tom-john didn't
let go.

"All hands witness punishments," Tom-john said
sadly, pulling me back around.

Whack!

My bile rose. I pulled free from my leather coat,
leapt to the mast, scurried down the rope ladder, and
made it to the rail just in time to barf over it. If anyone
noticed me I never knew; all that I saw was the rocking
sea, all that I felt was my guts heaving, and all that I
heard was the cracking of the cat and its companion
screams. I convulsed with every whack.

In the daze after the whipping, Mr. Roberts ordered
the keel-hauling. A long rope was tossed over the
bowsprit so that men both on the port and starboard
sides held one end. Untied from the cannon, limp as a
floating corpse, Keeler was carried forward. The pirates,
under close supervision by Mr. Roberts, tied one end of
the long rope to Keeler's wrists. The other end of the
rope was tied to Keeler's ankles. Mr. Roberts paused to
glance at Captain Beckett, who stood stern and
composed, watching intently. Quietly Captain Beckett
nodded.

Keeler was thrown overboard.

"Pull!" shouted a pirate, and I spied half-a-dozen
pirates tugging on the other end of the long rope on the
far side of the ship.

"Pull! Pull before he drowns!"

"Not so fast! You'll cut him to ribbons!"

Comprehension cascaded over me like the Silver Sprinkle: Keeler was being drug under the ship, against the wide, wooden hull, beneath the water, over the sharp barnacles. The Seahawk was a newer ship, but certainly there would be enough razor-edged barnacles to slit every inch of his skin as he was drug overtop them. How could Keeler survive? If he screamed underwater, even once, then he'd drown.

"Pull! For God's sake, pull!"

The pullers moved abaft along the rail; the current was adding to Keeler's injury, sweeping him along its underbelly at ten knots. One minute passed, and then a second. Several pirates swept off ragged hats and coifs and grimly bowed their heads. I trembled, clinging to the rail to keep from falling. Angela's cat had opened deep gashes across his back; the salt water in his wounds must be torturing Keeler.

I glanced at Angela, and for the first time I understood how she could lead men; Captain Angel stood unflinching beside Captain Beckett, her arms crossed under her breasts, her rigid expression resolute, her hand still clasping the bloody cat. She looked as unmovable as a mountain, staring at the pullers like everyone else. Not a trace of fear or doubt shadowed her granite frown.

"He's coming up! Pull!"

Anxious anticipation filled the crew. Keeler was pulled aboard rapidly, then dropped onto the deck. He looked flaccid, almost boneless. His clothes were shredded, and the seawater splashing from his many cuts ran pink like the waters of Gibbet Bay after a waylay.

"God almighty!"

"Like ground meat!"

"He's alive!"

A few pirates cheered, but not many. Some shrugged, then turned away in disgust. Others rushed forward, some eager to see Keeler's misery, some kneeling to gently help. Captain Beckett vanished into his cabin. Angela waited a moment, scanning the deck with her eyes, and paused on me. Ghastly pale, slightly green, vomit on my face, Angela held me long in her sight, and then she shook her head, almost imperceptively, and followed Captain Beckett into his quarters.

At dusk, Tom-john brought me stew and biscuits, but I couldn't eat. Even the news that Keeler was going to live didn't help much. I wanted to go home, but what then? All this fighting and killing; where had it gotten us? Wreckers had to live secretly, isolated on our cliffs over Gibbet Bay, unable to tolerate a single neighbor's visit. Our industry required our neighbors to think us madmen. These sea-pirates: were their lives any better? Pillaging and thieving away empty lives, homeless, betrayed by captains like Beckett and whipped into bloody fragments by Captain Angel; were any of them going to die happy?

"I think I'll go to sleep," I told Tom-john, trying not to smell his reeking stew-bucket.

"No," Tom-john said firmly. "Come."

The evening was blustery, chill, a sour end to a distasteful day. Tom-john lowered a long rope over the side and then led our way down the wide hull, motioning for silence. I wondered where we were going; never had Tom-john descended to the hull without his buckets. To my surprise, Tom-john stomped twice on a closed third-tier cannon port as if knocking. The port door instantly opened, and Tom-john vanished through it into the lower hull. One of the pirates, a grizzled old sea-rat whose chubby cheeks lay half-hidden by a short, thick white beard, stuck his head out of the cannon port and waved me forward with a friendly smile. Hesitantly, still gripping the rope, I scaled down the wooden hull, bounced off as the ship tilted, and then swung inside the port as it rocked back.

Hands seized me in the darkness. I fought against them, but Tom-john's voice warned me to be silent. They took my rope and tied it to a cannon, and then they closed the port door. A single lantern was uncovered, driving back the darkness. The lower gun deck was full of pirates, nine exactly; Angela's men. One man was laid out on old blankets on the floor; Keeler, although he was almost unrecognizable. Torn pages from a book papered him, each covering a slew of nasty gashes, blood tracing the lines of a hundred smaller cuts, soaked completely over the larger cuts. Keeler must've been dragged face-first against the hull; every inch of his skin looked like a pale tree that a bear had sharpened its claws upon.

"Give Tadpole a drink," the old salt said.

A bottle was passed to me and I drank a deep gulp. The rum burned, but I didn't care anymore. Still staring at Keeler, I took another.

"Easy, Tadpole," Tom-john warned. "Drunkards fall off the yards."

"Don't feel too sorry for him," the dwarf growled.

"Enough of that!" the old salt said.

"His mouth could've gotten us all keel-hauled!"

The old salt turned to me.

"Ignore Tenny, Tadpole," he said. "I'm Salty, and Captain Angel asked us to welcome you. This is Breakwater, Slim, Capsize, Zewdnesh, and Aidan."

I gazed at each of them as they were introduced. I'd seen them all before: Salty was the oldest of them, a grizzled sea-pirate with boney legs and a round pot-belly. Breakwater was small, rat-faced, and very dark-skinned, with long black hair, a wispy beard, and a greasy complexion with small, bright-red sores on his cheeks; he had a nasty sneer which made me think him a caitiff. Slim was very young and slender, perhaps the same age as Gerome David, but his pale skin was lobster-red and looked shiny, as if recently oiled. Slim had spring-green eyes and light, sandy hair; I'd noticed him before as the youngest pirate beside myself. Capsize was very fat, a giant of a man wearing a ragged violet vest over a thin shirt and holey trousers that exposed rolls of flesh that no one wanted to see. Zewdnesh was the weather-master, a black man which, before being shanghaied, I'd only sharked. Zewdnesh looked very old and tough, but he had relaxed, confidant brown eyes. Aidan had bright red-hair and a quiet, reserved look, as if he suspected that I was one of Captain Beckett's men. Aidan was thickly-built, perhaps an inch shorter than I, but with an angry glare in his dark green eyes. He had a short beard and still-healing wounds on his face and his left arm, which was bandaged with blood-crusted rags. Tenny was the midget, a short, round man, about Uncle Rory's age. He looked at me with a wry smile as if packed with humor, but his right hand was missing, his forearm ending in a sharp stump, and his right leg was thickly-bandaged.

"How's Keeler?" I asked.

"Bad," Salty said. "He's torn up front and back. This makes five trips under the hull for him ... and I couldn't count how many cattings. But he'll make it; Keeler's strong, and monstrous in a fight, worth three other men. His clenched fists resemble mauls; no one's ever beaten him at fisticuffs."

"Best let him sleep," Tom-john said.

"Aye, recovery takes time," Salty said, and he took the bottle from my hands and pulled a long swig, then passed it to Slim.

"Let's get comfortable," Tenny said, and he sat down on a cannon, wincing and grabbing his bandaged leg.

"What happened?" I asked him.

"Took a cutlass-point taking The Seahawk," Tenny scowled. "Wouldn't have if Captain Beckett had followed the Pact."

"Belay that!" Zewdnesh hissed. "Ships have ears."

"I was a gunner, the best, but without my hand I'm just a swab," Tenny said to me.

"A swab washes out a cannon after it fires, before reloading, so that the fresh powder doesn't ignite," Tom-john explained, and I tried to look impressed, although I'd known that all my life.

"Don't trust Tenny," Salty warned. "He's got a wicked sense of humor; once a fuse fizzled, and Tenny asked a new sailor to look down the mouth of the cannon to see if its ball was stuck."

"As ugly as he was, losing his head was an improvement," Tenny chuckled. Capsize smiled at his joke, but Slim scowled.

"I'm Slim," Slim re-introduced himself, passing the rum bottle to Tom-john before he shook my hand with his very-greasy palm. "Sorry about the coconut oil; I burn badly."

"Treasure glistens," Tenny chided.

"Don't call me Treasure," Slim snapped, but he didn't look angry. "I've been Captain Angel's man for over a year."

"Captain Angel's pretty Treasure," Tenny grinned.

Slim jumped forward, but the large, fat man stepped in his way, and Slim bounced off him. I stared at his chubby, smiling face hung with multiple chins.

"Ummmm... Capsize, wasn't it?"

"They call me Capsize because I can't swim," Capsize said, and he reached out a huge, flabby hand and shook mine. "I float, unfortunately upside-down, but ..." Capsize reached forward, grabbed my ribs, and lifted me with ease. "I'm the only man-jack that can hoist more than Keeler."

His strength, and the ease with which he lifted me, was startling, but Capsize set me down, still smiling, and then took the rum bottle from Tom-john.

"Tadpole, this is Zewdnesh, from Ethiopia," Tom-john said. "Zewdnesh is the best weather-master to ever sail."

Zewdnesh bowed slightly, almost formally, and I awkwardly bowed back.

"The clouds converse as they race past each other on the Great River East," Zewdnesh said in a slow, crisp voice. "You must listen closely to hear their words. I listen."

"That leaves only Aidan," Salty said, nodding to the Gaelic, red-haired man.

"Hey!" complained the small, rat-faced, black-haired man with the greasy, wispy beard.

"Quiet yourself!" Tenny ordered.

"Tadpole, this is Breakwater," Tom-john said, his voice full of disgust, gesturing to the rat-faced man. "He's one of our crewmates ..."

"Not mine!" Slim argued.

"Easy, lads," Salty said. "Breakwater's one of us now."

"He can't be trusted," Capsize said with a nasty glare at Breakwater.

"I'll be dead before any of you!" Breakwater argued.

"Enough!" Salty hissed. "One shout and Captain Beckett will personally ask us why we're here. Tadpole, Breakwater sailed with us on The Walrus Tusk with Captain Corker and on The Silver Enchantment. Few live to trust Breakwater twice, but he's trapped here with us. His reputation's so bad that Captain Beckett refused to accept his oath to The Seahawk; he said that Breakwater's word wasn't worth sea-foam. When Captain Beckett kills us, he'll start with Breakwater, and everyone knows it."

Breakwater's rat-faced scowl matched its description, and the hateful sneer between his pencil-thin mustache and a wispy beard, enhanced by the bright-red sores on his cheeks, only solidified my dislike. I made a mental note to be especially wary of Breakwater. Breakwater seized the rum and drank greedily as if to inure himself from contempt.

"Enough," Aidan said with a Gaelic accent, like Uncle Rory used to have, and he pulled the rum from Breakwater, took a short drink, and passed it back to me. "We're here to welcome Tadpole, not argue amongst ourselves."

"So, Angela ... Captain Angel ... ordered you to be nice to me?" I said, taking a deep drink. I hadn't meant my voice to be derisive but the pirates all scowled at this question.

"Captain Angel didn't order me to take you aloft," Tom-john said reprovingly.

"I know."

"Understand, Tadpole," Salty said. "Our lives are over once Captain Beckett gets enough treasure to replace us. I'd trust you just for Tom-john's sake, but your treasure map is our doom."

I apologized, but they waved me off. We got as comfortable as we could, sitting against the cannons and braces. Capsize settled against the hull; the boards creaked loudly under his great weight, such that Tenny and Slim shushed him. Capsize ignored them while Salty opened another bottle of rum and passed it around.

"Who are your friends in the hold?" Zewdnesh asked.

I lied quickly, briefly naming us all as farmers, and then asked how they were.

"Your uncle seems in good health," Zewdnesh said. "Your brother's fate blows on precarious winds. A storm is coming; the Great River East cries out."

"Great River East?"

"You have seen it all your life," Zewdnesh said slowly, his aged face lined with wind-burned wrinkles. "Lower clouds obey the four winds and buffet about like children. Higher clouds always flow eastwards on the Great Sky River; always eastwards."

"I never noticed."

"Fools look, wise men see," Zewdnesh said.

"Wise men aren't always right," Tenny said. "John Hawkins was a wise man, and look where he got us."

"John Hawkins?"

"Admiral Sir John Hawkins," Aidan said. "Slave trader, English shipbuilder, commander and navigator: in 1588, John Hawkins helped design ships fast enough to defeat the Spanish Armada, and he devised naval blockades to intercept Spanish treasure ships ... and pirates. John's father, William, was a confidant of Henry VIII."

"John Hawkins designed the first man-'o-war," Salty said. "He's to blame for the murder of thousands of pirates."

"That's why Captain Angel devised the Pact to capture The Seahawk," Slim said.

"She'd be in command if Captain Beckett had any honor," Aidan said.

"Belay that!" Salty hissed. "We'll all end up like Keeler ... or worse!"

"Captain Beckett controls all piracy in these waters now," Tenny said. "The Seahawk could take out a Naus with ease."

"What's a Naus?" I asked.

"A nau: a carrack, a three- or four-masted ship with a rounded stern and a fore and aftcastle, and a tall bowsprit," Salty explained. "The Portuguese called it a nau, and the Spanish call it a carraca. John Hawkins designed the first man-'o-war from the plans for a carrack."

"Carrack was a good line," Tom-john said.

"You think that anything with masts is a good ship," Tenny said.

"I've sailed them all," Salty said. "Barque, barquentine, brig, brigantine, topsail schooner, ketch, and frigate, but I've never felt anything like the deck of a man-'o-war."

"The draft alone alarms me," Aidan said. "I hear that they're making man-'o-wars now that are two hundred feet long and could have up to a hundred and twenty cannon: four guns fore, eight aft, and fifty-four on each side."

"The days of pirating are over," Salty scowled. "Used to be that any twenty determined men could commandeer a ship and make a good living. These big ships have killed us."

"Sounds good to me," Capsize said. "The bigger, the better."

"Any ship that you're on carries another foot of draft ... and bilge," Tenny sneered.

"Size of character," Capsize grinned.

"Not so preferable the last time that you splashed," Slim laughed. "We had to right you before you drowned."

All of the pirates laughed, even Capsize. I joined in, relaxing. I'd found good friends at last, but I had to keep reminding myself of Uncle Rory's instructions: if I said too much then I could kill us all, including Angela and her men. I had to stay sober and say as little as possible.

Jay Palmer

10

GOD'S THUMPS

Aloft, I clung tight to the main mast as the wind whistled past my red, chapped ears, which stung and felt dried and cracked. The wind had blown hard all day; twice we'd altered course, but to no avail; the sea-scent was strong and sharp, its humidity filled with a bitter, acrid tang. I'd lived on sea-cliffs too long not to recognize those signs; Zewdnesh had been right: a storm was coming. I wondered how he'd known of it yesterday, if he'd truly heard the winds speaking.

The Seahawk was pitching roughly, harder than I'd thought a big ship could. The mounting waves punched against our hull like giant fists, shivering the timbers and vibrating every mast and spar, which strained the rigging as the taut sails pushed us forward, desperately trying to escape the threatening tumult shoving us in ever-faster thrashings, but not fast enough. Thick dark clouds crept overtop us like a billowy black quilt being drawn over the sky.

Delighted, Tom-john swung back and forth on a rope between the masts, his face jubilant, cheering wildly. I considered abandoning him and crawling into the safety of the hull, but Uncle Rory's orders echoed in my head; I'd caused our ruin once, and he'd kill me if I did it again. I needed to stay as far away from Captain Beckett's pirates as possible, and if that meant that I had to stay up here with Tom-john in the middle of a storm, then that's what I'd do. How terrible could it be? Tom-john loved it, and he'd survived many storms. I was wrapped in the heavy coat that he'd given me, and if I stayed low in the crowfoot and clung tight, then my chances of survival were far better than his.

Twice I saw Angela nervously pacing the rocking deck with a mastery born only of long experience on ships being tossed by waves. Both she and Mr. Roberts kept shouting at the men, who were lashing down everything, preparing for the sea's oncoming assault. One cannon came loose and rolled across the deck; a fat pirate, one of Captain Beckett's men, got knocked over by its collision, then screamed that his leg was broken. Angela demanded to know who'd lashed the loose cannon down, and when a swarthy pirate from The Red Pantheon was pointed out by his fellows, Angela's cat made him howl as it struck across his back amid a mad dive to escape her anger. Only Captain Beckett's shouted command stayed further punishments, ordering all hands back to work, but he added that the time for punishment would come. The swarthy pirate blanched, but helped the others push the cannon back into place and batten it down tightly.

The wind strengthened; sudden gusts forced me to cling to the thin wooden rail around the crowfoot, terrified of being tossed off. Salt-spray lashed my face, although I was far above the water-line. Between the fierce shakes and trembles of the ship, I seized and tucked in the corners of my bulky coat and blanket, which the wind was catching and blowing about with a fearfully-strong grip.

Tom-john's laughter filled my ears during the moments when the whistling winds slackened.

"Tadpole!" Tom-john cried. "Stand up! Feel the power of God!"

Tom-john swung to the crowfoot, clinging with ease and confidence as the mast tilted wildly, the pitching ship trembling. His eyes were bright and eager, his smile exuberant, and his lively excitement as the ship swayed almost made him look like he was dancing.

"No, no; you'll lose your blanket that way," he said. "Here, take off your coat."

Tom-john was crazy, but he knew what he was doing, so I didn't resist. He pulled me up and removed my coat, then spread my wide blanket around my shoulders so that it hung behind me like a cape. Tugging hard, he pulled the blanket's front two corners down to my waist, making the rest of the blanket bunch tightly around my neck in thick wool folds over my shoulders. Then, making me hold the front ends of my blanket in place with one hand, then the other, he helped me pull on my great leather coat over the bulky wool blanket, which bulged ridiculously and felt terrible. I felt like a hunchback, and probably looked stupid, but Tom-john smiled approvingly.

"That'll keep most of you dry and warm, at least until manhood bulks you up. You're a brave lad, Tadpole; the other sailors will respect you for this, if you weather God's attention." Tom-john pointed a stubby finger to the horizon, a dark, frothing sea of milky-white caps under thick, black clouds that promised heavy rain. "See? God himself comes to bless us!"

Through the flaring winds, I looked at the approaching storm, and saw only death. The sea was huge, vaster than I'd ever realized, the mighty Seahawk only a tiny leaf floating upon it. I feared that none of us would survive the day. Grandpa Barnaby had told us kids terrible tales of storms at sea, but none of them left me as frightened as I felt now, and the grasping hands of this storm had yet to close upon us.

The prospect of earning the respect of Captain Beckett's pirates didn't reassure me; if Uncle Rory's plan worked, then they'd all be dead soon. But Tom-john, Angela, Salty, and the rest did matter; I wondered what Grandpa Jack would say to them. Normally, only Wreckers were allowed to leave Gibbet Bay, but surely he would understand that these pirates had helped us and saved Gerome David's life. Since Grandpa Barnaby had once been a pirate himself, he'd look upon them as kindred souls.

"Take a swing, lad; there's a true bucko!"

Tom-john stuck the rope in my hands. At first I pushed it back, refusing, but Tom-john shoved me over the rail with surprising strength, and I seized the rope before I toppled down onto the deck, and then I swung wildly out into the capricious winds. The rope burned my hands, but I clung tightly as the rocking of the ship tossed me about like a helpless toy on a string. Childishly crying aloud, I flew out over the side, beyond the safety of the rail, over the deadly frothing caps. Then The Seahawk tilted suddenly, jerking me backwards as the mast yanked. I screamed, suddenly flung out over the rail on the other side, again hanging palely over a violent sea-grave which would suck me down if my knotted fingers loosed upon my only lifeline. Then the ship pitched again and I was jerked back. I kicked out as I was thrown back, my boot skimmed the fully-billowed main sail. Desperately I glanced about for any line that I could catch my foot on, anything to end this nightmare. My hands strained to cling tight, the rope burning indelibly into my grip; one slip and I'd never be heard from again.

"Tom-john!" Angela cried from far below. "No hands overboard!"

"Aye, aye!" Tom-john shouted back, and as the ship tilted again, the wild wind tossed me about like a helpless spider on a broken web. Suddenly a hand of iron seized my coat and drug me to the mizzen mast. I seized its wooden solidity with a deathgrip, frozen as if part of its wooden surface, feeling flooding relief in its strength despite the rocking of the ship and the strained flexing that I could feel from within the tall mast.

"Well done, me hearty!" Tom-john laughed and, ignoring my terror, he pulled the thin rope from my clenched hands, and suddenly Tom-john leapt out into open air upon my rope with a playful shout. Instantly he inverted as the long rope snapped taut and, upside-down, Tom-john swung low over the deck, sweeping its surface with a jovial laugh.

Several pirates jump aside to avoid Tom-john bowling them over. Mr. Roberts and those pirates cursed and shouted many names at Tom-john, but the others only laughed. Angela said nothing, just looked at Captain Beckett, who stood without his hat, as still as a statue against the buffeting wind, observing everything, his long matted beard blowing about wildly. He glanced up and saw me standing on the spar, clutching the mizzen mast for dear life. No expression crossed his face, merely a gaze of serious interest, as if calculating my worth. I understood his estimation; Tom-john was a valuable asset, a fearless pirate willing to risk his life when any sane sailor would be huddling inside the ship's belly and praying for God's pardon. Perhaps Captain Beckett thought that I'd make a good replacement for Tom-john, once he didn't need Angela or her men anymore. Captain Beckett stared at me for a long moment, then turned away; I wasn't worth much of his attention.

I watched the other pirates, Capsize the biggest of them, busy tying down the last of our loads; Capsize held everything still while the others lashed them down. When satisfied, Mr. Roberts reported to the captain, and then he ordered all of the men below to secure the lower guns. They hurried down the stairs as if fighting to escape the certain death of remaining above deck. Longingly I watched the last of them descend. I'd much prefer to wait out the storm inside the safety of the hull, but up here, while my life was endangered, Uncle Rory and Gerome David's lives were spared; the more time that I spent with Captain Beckett's blackguards, the greater the likelihood that I'd slip up. Captain Beckett had promised us slow, painful deaths if the Cave of Riches turned out to hold nothing but the Golden Twinkle; he would certainly keep that oath.

Captain Beckett calmly walked toward his cabin door. Angela followed him, but she momentarily paused and glanced up at me before entering. Her strong, pretty face had piercing eyes that coldly drilled into my heart, more frightening than any storm, and they seemed to flash before she closed the door behind her.

Ka-BOOM!

The sudden concussion of thunder deafened me. The force of it blasted me down and crackled across my skin; never had I felt lightning so close or stayed outside on the sea cliffs during a lightning storm. I started to shake and whimper; *I couldn't do this.*

A solid body collided with me and Tom-john shouted in my ear.

"Come, Tadpole: back home."

He wrapped his strong arm around me, but I clung tightly to the mast.

"You can't weather God's presence here. You're too young; one breath of God would toss your skinny bones to Davy Jones without a thought or a care. Come; I'll see you safely over."

Frightened, but trusting to Tom-john, I released the tilting mast. Tom-john lifted me with ease, then jumped hard and far into open air. I cried out, flailing my arms and legs, but Tom-john clutched me tightly and swung far out, around the main mast. The white waves crashed below us, already double in size and force, before we swung back. Tom-john twisted and thrashed, making our swing lead us toward the foremast, which he barely caught with the toe of his boot before our momentum tossed us past the deck and out over the starboard sea. We tightly grabbed at the flailing lines bound to the foremast above and below, and then climbed down to the crowfoot, which I greeted with trepidatious relief. Tom-john sat me down between the thin rails, then folded my leather coat tightly about me. Out of one pocket Tom-john pulled a thin, wide scrap of soft leather, which he bound tightly about my head like a woman's scarf. Finally Tom-john drew out a stout length of thin rope.

"Only God and the helmsman are left to watch us," Tom-john shouted to be heard. "Brave swings on ropes are fun, and impress the men, but now's the time for caution."

Tom-john bound the thin rope around me, slipping it between the rungs of the tiny rail, lashing me down, and twice wrapped it around my chest and the sturdy foremast at my back. He finished his tight bindings with the mystery knot; he didn't want me untying it.

"Stay here," Tom-john ordered, and I nodded worriedly; his mystery knot gave me little choice. I wasn't going anywhere unless I took the whole mast with me, a thought that I didn't find comforting. "The rain's coming; it's gonna be rough. If God calls, then I'll speak to him for you."

Tom-john patted my thick, blanket-padded shoulder, then stood up, despite the fierce wind, and gripped the long rope.

"Where are you going?" I asked, shouting through the gusts.

Tom-john glanced knowingly at me, a half-frown on his face.

"That's between God and me, Tadpole."

With a fearless swing, Tom-john left me alone. I watched his shape fly far out, over the churning waves, then circle out of sight behind the main sail. Then a flash of lightning blazed, illuminating the black, threatening clouds like a sudden spark in a deep cave; an instant's view quickly stolen by darkness. Our shadowed white sheets suddenly blazed like a bright, snowy hillside, then vanished back into storm-wracked shadow. The Seahawk lurched, tilted forward, and the splash of an ocean wave washed the deck. Salt-froth sprayed upwards, splashing onto me. I was already wet; the fierce wind was slashing droplets off of the waves like rain from all directions. I shifted my position, keeping my grip tight upon the tiny wooden rail, which had once seemed sturdy but now looked terrifyingly frail, torn between fighting to free myself and blessing the spider web of rope holding me safe. Across the sea, I saw a vast, dark curtain; heavy rain was already falling less than a mile away.

The dark curtain of rain overtook us hard and abruptly, hammering like a giant waterfall. The rain pelted unusually cold, and I ducked to protect my face from its icy talons. The gusty winds seemed to slacken as the sudden deluge poured upon us, after which I was suddenly glad for the leather scrap tied over my head. However, the water streamed down the sides of my face and neck into my coat; a liquid chill leaked down my shoulders, inside of my coat, onto my bare chest. I twisted and shifted as best I could, stretching out my chin to capture and close the wide, wool-stuffed gap of my coat's leather collar, vainly attempting to seal the water's entrance.

The wind suddenly whipped into life like a striking hydra, firing rain like gravel from a blunderbuss, shooting from all directions. Iron-hard droplets stung my face, and I let go of the shaking rails to shield my eyes, crying out against the thrashing of the ship, its sudden rises and plummets, and its thunderous crashes as it fell from towering crest to Hellish trough.

"Spare the sheets!"

Pirates raced out into the storm and scrambled up the shrouds. One, whom I recognized as Pete, suddenly appeared at my side. He was already drenched.

"What is it?" I cried.

Pete looked at me, helplessly bound, and a wry smirk twisted his rain-wet lips.

"The sails must be saved!" Pete shouted back.

"Let me out!" I shouted, struggling against my bonds.

Pete ignored me and climbed past. I shouted, but he and thirteen other pirates climbed past me, heedless save for their sarcastic laughs. Darkness hid their faces, save for the blinding flashes of lightning so close that their thunderclaps seemed to precede them. I cursed them with names that Mother would've slapped me for using. They climbed above me as I struggled, realizing just how expertly Tom-john had bound me, my fingers, numbed by cold, vainly clawing at the mystery knot which, now soaked, seemed even more impossible to untie.

The sails loosed and flapped wildly over my head; they were furling all of the sheets. I should be out there helping; I was just as much a pirate as they were, if not as good a sailor. I felt ashamed and childish, staying bound, helpless, while the men worked.

I considered just wriggling out; I was slender and dexterous. Certainly I could escape without untying the ropes, but then I'd have to slide clear out of the bulky coat that helped restrain me, and it could take twenty minutes; they'd be done in ten.

A strangled cry rose above the howling wind. Far over my head, one pirate had fallen. He hung from the end of a main spar one-handed as his fellows raced toward him. The ship rocked and tilted; surely the man would've been lost overboard, but suddenly Tom-john came flying down out of the rainstorm, a rope knotted under his arms, and he seized the hanging sailor tightly around his waist. Rather than pull him up, one pirate clutched the hanging sailor by his forearm and Tom-john held firm to his waist, while another quickly tied a stout rope around his wrist. This seemed to be expected; when finished, they all released their grips at once, and the man plummeted ten feet, crying out as the tightening rope jerked hard on his arm, then swung him to the foremast right over my head. One-handed, the man seized and clutched the mast desperately, still crying out. No one rushed to his aid, the other pirates returned to the spars, hurrying to save the wet sails which this violent wind would surely shred. Tom-john remained hanging where he was until, by himself, he had the whole port side of the huge sail furled and secured, and then he pushed off, flying out over the wild sea to the main mast.

"Are you alright?" I shouted to the rescued sailor who'd nearly fallen overboard, who was still clutching to the foremast, his boots barely resting on the thick rope binding that still covered where the mast had been shattered by a cannonball.

"My shoulder's out!" he cried, pain wracking his voice into a plea, but I couldn't get free to help. I reached up with both hands and pushed against his boots from below, helping to support his weight.

Straining to hold him, I tilted my head back until I could see behind me; the main mast and mizzen mast were alive with pirates, half of the sails furled, bound to their spars, some sheets already torn; the mizzen topsail showed two wide rents. Sailors climbed like spiders through the buffeting winds and storm-hurled rain, which struck your face like fistfuls of musket-shot. These pirates didn't look frightening now; terror masked their faces, horror of the furious squall overhead and the churning, watery grave beneath. Yet they climbed quickly, constantly shouting to each other, until every sail was tied to its spar, and then they scrambled back down to the safety of the deck, vanishing almost instantly into the dark depths of the hull. Pete and another helped the wounded man that I was supporting, and then they crawled down past me, carrying him, without a word. Soon they were all gone, save Tom-john, the helmsman who was struggling to man the great wheel, and I. Even Mr. Roberts had fled to the safety of the cabins.

"God's here!"

Tom-john's smiling face loomed before mine.

"Untie me!"

Tom-john shook his head. I noticed that all of the feathers had blown out of his hatband, which now looked bare and plain, strapped even tighter to his head. He looked drenched inside and out.

"This wind's too great!" Tom-john shouted. "You'd be in Davy Jones if you'd tried to help. Look up: see the face of God!"

Lightning flashed, arcing around all sides of The Seahawk at once, as if we were a drowning bird in an electric cage. Thunder boomed, silencing all other sounds and thrumming painfully in my ears.

"We'll be killed!" I shouted angrily.

Tom-john smiled widely.

"Where better to die than before the eyes of God?"

"Untie me!"

Tom-john lifted up two separate ropes that had been blowing about him, and I realized that both ropes were bound tight about him, one under his arms, tied in a thick knot over his chest, the other about his waist.

"No one escapes God's attention without lifelines!" Tom-john shouted to be heard over the gusting wind. "You're doing fine. Stay here. God sees you!"

Tom-john didn't jump off, but carefully climbed, more slowly than ever, over my head and up the foremast. I shouted repeatedly, demanding that he come back, stay low, do anything but act crazy, but Tom-john ignored me. He scaled to a main line between the foremast and the main mast, shimmied across it, tossed by the wind, and finally reached the main mast; now I knew that he was crazy. He tied another rope about his waist, released one of the two that he'd already had, and then he started to climb again. I shouted at him, knowing that he couldn't hear me, but certain that he was going to get himself killed. Lightning struck every second, the boom of one thunderclap still echoing when the next erupted.

I struggled against my bonds, helplessly flailing, to no avail. The storm grew worse, wilder, raging with a fury unmatched by mortal vehemence. Waves rose and crashed over the deck, splashing froth so high that buckets of saltwater slapped my face all the way up in the crowfoot. I cried out, awash in terror, like a child trapped in a stormy nightmare. The sea boiled and frothed and churned, revealed in horrifying flashes that threatened to reach down and stab us with burning death. I stared, disbelieving that any ship could survive such an oceanic Hell, a hurricane of violence and destruction beneath which The Seahawk struggled like a fragile, empty egg shell bobbing feebly on wild waves, eventually to be crushed. No man could survive this evil; if The Seahawk sank, then we'd all be dead.

I glanced back at the helm. No pilot stood there now. The deck was awash, seawater streaming back and forth as the storm-tossed ship lurched wildly, side to side, fore to aft, steerless in the wind. Whether the helmsman had fled inside or been washed overboard I couldn't say but, looking up, I spied the craziest sight of all. Tom-john was at the top of the main mast, clinging to the jack spar below the long, whipping, streaming pendant, waving one bare hand overhead as high as he could reach, utter delight beaming from his face as the ship tilted wildly, riding the rigging like a bull-rider while lightning struck from all around.

Seconds lasted hours and hours stretched to eternities. Calmness settled on me eventually; amid my incoherent screams, a subtle, soft whisper patiently explained that I couldn't get any more frightened, which seemed strangely reassuring. Even the greatest sailor was at the mercy of God during a storm like this, and nothing that I did, and no matter where I tried to hide on this ship, my power to command my own fate was insignificant. In this storm, I was as safe here as anywhere that I could get to. If I had to die, then I'd rather drown beside Uncle Rory and my beloved brother, but trying to get to them now would put me at far greater risk, and I could almost hear Uncle Rory's enraged admonitions if I dared untie myself from the mast in the middle of a tempest just to die beside them. He'd box my ears for sure, assuming that I had any left by the time that I made it to his side. I hunkered down inside my leather coat, which couldn't have gotten wetter if I'd been swimming, inside of which the cold rain had pooled, partially kept at bay by the thick wool folds that Tom-john had forced upon me. My boots were full of water, and I was chilled to the bone, but there was nothing left to do. Around me, the gale rose in ever-increasing vehemence and I cowered and tried to sleep.

The sun broke through the remaining clouds like the grace of God shining upon a calm sea. I wearily opened my eyes, not sure if I'd fallen asleep, passed out from exhaustion, or fainted from fear.

"Easy! Slow!"

Voices startled me; I twisted around and spied several pirates already in the heights working the lines. A still form hung from two ropes, one from the foremast, one from the main: Tom-john hung unconscious, his arms and legs limply dangling below him.

"Let me free!" I shouted, and the men saw me. Slicer came over and dropped onto the tiny crowfoot, standing over me, one foot upon the rail on each side. He glanced at Tom-john's mystery knot and frowned, fingered it curiously, and then he reached inside his dry jacket and brought out a small, sharp knife; he easily sliced the rope in half. Freed, I started untying the rest of Tom-john's half hitches and slip knots until I could stand. As I rose, two quarts of water, trapped inside my coat, splashed down upon my wet trousers and rain-filled boots. I struggled to quickly peel off my wet leather coat, soaked blanket, drenched shirt and sopping boots, but they clung tight, holding me like chains. While I struggled, I admired with relief the smooth, even green sea around us, which had grown delightfully calm, and the blue sky peeking through the remnants of the white puffy clouds. But I couldn't rest; Tom-john was hurt. I quickly climbed down to the deck, worried beyond words.

Supine in the center of the deck, Tom-john lay like a dead man. I stepped to his side, but one of the pirates seized and held me back.

"Best not touch him, boy," said a pirate. "He's still breathing, but barely alive. He's been struck by lightning again, the madman."

I looked up at the pirate, who was both older and bigger than I, and clenched my fists.

"Belay that!" Captain Beckett commanded. "Fighters kiss the gunner's daughter, and Angela wields the cat-of-nine."

I stared up at Captain Beckett. He stood tall and commanding, unbreachably strong, beside Angela, and surrounded by his crew. The gold of his brightly trimmed purple jacket and spotless white shirt shined in the renewing sun. Angela's eyes flashed at me warningly, but I couldn't let Tom-john, my only friend, die. I glanced about desperately, spied a large dagger sheathed on the belt of the pirate holding me, and I snatched his weapon free; I slashed viciously at the crowd, not trying to cut anyone, but forcing them back. Even Captain Beckett's eyes flew open and he stepped back.

"I'm going to get my uncle," I said to Captain Beckett. "Uncle Rory's a great man; very wise. He can help Tom-john; I know it."

Everyone stood frozen, eyeing me warily. I had no hope of survival if these pirates rushed me, but I didn't care. I stared angrily at them, holding out my tiny knife as if I'd kill them all.

Captain Beckett calmly drew his sword and held it out at me; its point extended far past my reach, resting its sharp tip against my naked chest. I stared at him; he could run me through in an instant. Tears started in my eyes and I lowered the useless knife.

"Please; he's my friend."

"By all means," Captain Beckett said, a wry grin widening his narrow face. "Your uncle's in the hull, at the very bottom, I believe. Fetch him, if he can help; I need Tom-john."

At a wave from Angela, all of the pirates stood aside, opening a pathway to the stairs. With a distrustful glance at Captain Beckett, I turned and ran.

"Let him go," Captain Beckett ordered, and then I was crashing down the stairs, barefoot, slapping the boards as I nearly fell. On the third level, I stole a lit lantern from the hands of a surprised pirate, Aidan, realizing too late that he was one of Angela's men, who stumbled backwards as I unexpectedly pointed my deadly, stolen dagger at him. I took his lantern and continued down the last stair into the deep hold.

"Uncle!" I shouted.

Uncle Rory rose to his feet, shielding his eyes from the light of my lantern.

"Jeremy Albert?"

"You're needed on deck," I said, panting. "Tom-john ... was hit by lightning."

Uncle Rory stared at the dagger in my hand.

"He's still alive?"

"Yes. Captain Beckett told me to bring you. Hurry!"

Uncle Rory stared at me, taking in my unease and urgency.

"Give me the knife," Uncle Rory said. "I'll go up. You stay here ... with your brother."

I quickly offered everything that I held to Uncle Rory, but he took only the knife, leaving me the lantern. Without a word, he walked past me and climbed the stairs. I watched him go, terribly afraid for Tom-john.

"So ... my little brother's ... a pirate."

Startled, I almost dropped the lantern. Gerome David was sitting up, staring at me, one hand holding his stomach. Gerome David looked appalling, pale as a waterlogged corpse and twice as limp, but alive.

"You're still here?" I smiled.

Gerome David grinned; the effort seemed to tax him mightily.

"Don't ... get any ... ideas," Gerome David tried to chuckle. "I can still ... stand you on ... your head ... anytime."

"Sure," I humored him, too happy to care who insulted who. *My brother wasn't dead!* "You look uglier than usual."

"If I get ... any worse ... I'll look like ... you."

We both laughed, but then Gerome David started coughing, and I knelt and steadied him, worried. He seemed weaker than poor, bedridden Grandma Lydia, whose skin was papery-thin, but she was not nearly as pale as Gerome David. Uncle Rory had kept him alive; I was certain that he'd do the same for Tom-john.

"What ... happened?" Gerome David asked.

"We survived the storm," I said, and I glanced about to make sure that we were alone and then continued. "We've gotten both markers; our next stop is home."

"Too big," Gerome David said. "Man-'o-war ... too big. Family ... can't fight ... two hundred and ..."

"We don't have two hundred," I said. "We've got sixty-six, and some of them are on our side."

"Sixty-six?"

"After the capture of The Seahawk, Captain Beckett had forty-two, Angela had nine, and we got another fifteen from Captain Godsworth."

Gerome David frowned and looked skeptically at me, then gently shook his head.

"You're ... an idiot."

"Maybe, but you'd have to learn everything Uncle Rory knows just to reach idiot," I said. "We have allies, and we'll need them inside Gibbet Bay."

"We ... should die," Gerome David said, "for ... the family."

"It's too late for that," I said. "They have the bible and the map; they don't need us anymore."

A creaking board warned us; I stood and stared. Angela stepped out of the alcove of the stairs.

"Interesting conversation," Angela said. "Allies; that's an odd term for prisoners to use of their captors."

I stared, afraid, wondering how much she'd overheard. Angela stepped into the open, her pistol pointed at us.

"Please," I said. "Don't shoot."

"Why should I shoot?" Angela asked, stepping toward us, a mischievous smile on her face. "You're a smart lad, Tadpole."

"Tadpole ...?" Gerome David asked.

"Nothing," I snapped at him, and then I turned to Angela. "All that we want is to get to land and go free."

"So you say," Angela said. "Your uncle says even more, and yet he keeps silent when he chooses, more than you do. He's an impressive man; he'd make a great sailor."

"Pirate," I corrected her.

Angela smiled, a bright, cheery grin which lightened her beautiful face even in the pale, flickering lantern light, yet no trace of innocence glowed from her. She walked up to me, taller than I, her long hair hanging down over firm breasts bulging upwards from the tight brown leather vest that she wore, her two other pistols and her leather cat in her belt, and her three daggers sheathed, sewn into the tops of her tall boots. She stared at me, and then glanced down at Gerome David, who stared up at her amazed.

"We have a deal, if you recall," Angela said to me.

"Aye, Captain Angel, my captain," I said.

Captain Angel stole another glance at Gerome David, and then offered me her pistol. I held out my hand and she laid the loaded pistol into it.

"Captain Beckett?" I surmised.

"Right as we sail into the treasure-harbor," Captain Angel said. "I can't kill him, not if I mean to take command. I'll strand you, Rory, and your brother in this Cave of Riches whether we find treasure or not. Of course, you do have another choice."

"Join your crew," I guessed.

"Jeremy, shut up!" Gerome David hissed.

We both glanced at him, but only for a second. Though so weak that he could barely lift his head, Gerome David glared up at Angela as if he had the strength to resist her even when healed. I shook my head and stuck the pistol into my belt, its cold barrel against my hip.

"I saved your brother," Angel said, ignoring Gerome David. "I gave Rory the medicines that he needed. Without me, they'd both have died of wounds, infection, starvation, and dehydration; I kept my part of our bargain."

"At your signal, I kill Captain Beckett," I promised.

Angela stared into my eyes until I thought I'd break against her like surf on rocks, and then she reached out a strong, yet very feminine hand. Her finger brushed tenderly against my cheek, then softly slid down my throat, drawing an imaginary line with one hard fingernail down my naked chest with a red-hot fire like a knife-blade drawn straight from a forge.

"You're a very pretty boy," Captain Angela whispered. "Do you know how I started out as a pirate? As a ship-whore, my back against the hull, any man-jack atop me for half of his harbor dues. Being a pirate isn't easy, but it's free; you can become anything that you want, if you're smart enough, and determined, no matter what the cost. I've scars on my back from the cat in my belt, yet I've never wavered, and I took charge whenever I could, no matter how dangerous it seemed. You're clever, Jeremy Albert Wrecker. You're also a great shot, and I hear that your brother's just as good; you could both be captains of your own ships, which I could help you capture. But I must have The Seahawk, and if you fail me, if you even shoot and miss, then I'll kill you myself. I've killed far more men than you ..."

"I doubt that," I interrupted.

Angela smiled, a wide, wicked grin under her dark, narrowed eyes.

"My captaincy offers pleasures not had on any other ship," Angela said, and she placed her fiery, hard-nailed finger under my chin and raised my face. Her beautiful face loomed close; she kissed me, a soft, brief touch of searing lips, and then she quickly walked away toward the stairs.

"Shoot when I signal."

Angela was gone.

11

ANGELA'S LASH

"Tell me about Captain Angel."

Tom-john hesitated, looking up from the reverse-clove hitch that he was teaching me to tie. A bright grin widened his face. He glanced around, checking that the shrouds below us were empty. Tom-john was shirtless, his left shoulder tightly bandaged, his wounded arm set in a sling by Uncle Rory, who'd been granted full access to the deck in his new position as ship's surgeon. The pirates had cheered this promotion; many were still nursing open wounds from the capture of The Seahawk. Uncle Rory had been assigned a cabin, and he carried Gerome David up to rest in it, and Uncle Rory started seeing to the many badly-healed sword-cuts and the punctures of crudely-removed musketballs. Tom-john took another drink from his full bottle of rum, which Uncle Rory had prescribed and Captain Beckett had provided, for the pain of his burn, which covered his whole left shoulder where the lightning had struck him. However, when he turned back to me, confident that we wouldn't be overheard, his smile was brighter than ever.

"My beloved, bonnie Captain Angel!" Tom-john said. "What can I say? Angela's a warm wind that fills eager sails and tears all sheets too weak to restrain her. Even the greatest poetry isn't worthy of my precious betrothed, the love of my life. Angela is all that I ask of God."

"Then ... you're engaged."

"Engaged? Not formally, but such is customary among pirates; a bucko's life be full of risks. My Angela can't gamble her captaincy by public displays of favor. We're pledged, but untrophlighted."

"Then ... how do you know ...?"

The first hint of anger that I'd ever seen flushed Tom-john's rough, ruddy face, narrowed his eyes, and his grin vanished.

"Captain Angel is too great for any man not chosen by God."

The soft intensity in his voice warned me that I'd strayed into dangerous waters.

"I ... I'm sorry; that's not what I meant," I said quickly.

Tom-john flinched as he leaned forward, straining his shoulder, testing its range.

"Should I call Uncle Rory?"

"No, God's thumped me far worse than this."

"What did it feel like?"

"Can't say," Tom-john said as he carefully leaned back, moving judiciously. "Pain, fire; God's pure will is too great for mortal flesh. Yet it's exhilarating, as if the force of a thousand lives were coursing through you in one blinding, Heavenly moment. The deck-crawlers call me mad, but God will remember me when my boots stand before his throne. Good friends we are, or he would've killed me five mighty thumps gone by, but great plans has God for his bravest sailor."

"What plans?"

"Angela," Tom-john smiled widely again. "Captain Angel, his greatest creation; I am the gift that God has made to reward the proof of his supremacy, my beautiful, blessed Angela. Who else would be worthy of her but the bravest man alive?"

"No one," I assured him, certain that any other response would evoke bitter fury. Despite being wounded by a lightning strike, Tom-john was still incredibly strong and an unparalleled rigging-master; if angered, he could toss me overboard at will.

I glanced to the foremast and saw my heavy leather coat bound to the rail of the crowfoot, still drying out in the sun. My boots lay beside it, also soaked; it might take days for them to dry out completely. Many of the pirates were similarly undressed; vests and shirts lay about the shrouds like ragged flags blowing in the wind. But my coat was different; inside its deep pockets I'd stashed my pistol, my tool for killing Captain Beckett.

Would Angela keep her promise? Doubts gnawed. I'd killed many times, been taught to kill since I was six when I'd first caved in a merchantman's head with a rock that I'd tossed from the top of Gibbet Bay during my first waylay. But always I'd killed from a safe distance; sailors in Gibbet Bay couldn't scale its sheer cliffs, and the sailors aboard Captain Godsworth's ship couldn't walk across open sea. Killing a man aboard a ship that I was on seemed less certain; successful or not, all of Captain Beckett's pirates could scale the shrouds in seconds, and one pistol couldn't defeat them all. Musketballs were notoriously non-fatal instantly. Often victims of musket-fire suffered mortal wounds; Captain Beckett could give orders to kill me before his wounds proved mortal. When I fired at him, I'd have little time to aim, and my one shot had to kill instantaneously. His head was my best target, but he always wore that wide-brimmed hat, which would make shooting him from above very uncertain.

"I meant: how did Angela become captain?"

"Oh," Tom-john smiled, his usual manner returning. "I told you of the bad days; man-'o-wars hunting down every pirate ship; schooner, frigate, and merchantman. Dark times; no port was safe in daylight, supplies were scarce, and hungry pirates make mean crews. All sailors fear bad luck, and a woman aboard ship is terribly unlucky, so the whores are kept deep in the hold when they were allowed aboard at all. But Angela refused to stay imprisoned; whenever battle came, Angela stormed onto deck, and stole a saber or pike from one of the fallen, and then fought beside us like a sea-demon. Our enemies always laughed to see a woman pirate ... until one of them died laughing. Then a new man-'o-war, Poseidon's Avenger, chased us into a reef dotted with many tiny islands; bare rocks with many caves. When a rogue cannonball shattered our rudder chain, The Walrus Tusk, our beautiful ship, sailed onto a shallow reef and splintered. I was hurled overboard by the collision, but while Poseidon's Avenger peppered us from a safe distance, Angela led the dropping of the lifeboats behind the hull, and she herself fished me out of the sea.

"We escaped into a tiny sea-cave, and then fled to a different cave each night, under the dark of the moon, for Poseidon's Avenger patrolled those islands twice every day, hunting for the last of us. Shipless, Captain Corker dead, Angela led us to the outskirts of a poor fishing village. One cold, foggy morning, we rowed our skiffs in before dawn, just as the fishermen were awakening in the first light of morning to sift the sea for substance. Following Angela, we boarded and took their fisher, and afterwards, the men unanimously voted Angela as captain, and quickly she proved herself. Within a week, we'd waylaid, and took as our own, a full schooner: The Silver Enchantment, which Captain Beckett sank after we captured The Seahawk."

"How long did she captain The Silver Enchantment?"

"A year and a half," Tom-john smiled. "Quite a ship we had; grog at every meal and music every night. Many laughed at us for boasting a woman captain, but Angel proved her mastery over men and ships; never did any pirates gather so much plunder with so few losses. Her reputation grew; some ships simply offered us protection dues, and Captain Angela always kept her promises ..."

"Always?" I asked. "Angela never betrayed anyone?"

Tom-john eyed me knowingly, then glanced around again to make certain that no other hand was in the sheets.

"Tadpole, if my bonnie Angela says that you won't be harmed for your obligations, then you can bank your life on it. Mind your duty, and fail her not; Captain Angel plans around other men's minds like seagulls fly around masts. Seldom do any grasp her full plans, but all who prove loyal to her receive rewards beyond their wildest dreams."

That afternoon, as the last grimy pirate departed Uncle Rory's cabin with a fresh, clean bandage upon his right leg, the only scrap of clean cloth on him, I descended to the deck and entered his door.

"Articulate naught!" Uncle Rory hissed between clenched teeth. I froze, but he motioned for me to enter and close the door.

Uncle Rory's cabin was larger than most, though only a quarter of the space that Captain Beckett enjoyed.

Two stout wooden chairs sat before a sturdy table under shelves laden with many knives, a short saw, half-filled bottles, and many wax-sealed jars. The table was piled with ragged cloths, pushed aside to make room for a stained ink bottle and a red-bound book that Uncle Rory was writing in.

Gerome David was sitting up on the edge of the sole bed, a bucket of soapy water on the floor between his feet; he seemed to be washing rags. Beside him lay a large pair of scissors, and hanging from every possible surface all around the room were long, damp, carefully-cut bandages, newly-washed and set out to dry. Gerome David raised one finger to his lips and silently shushed me, and then pointed at the back wall. Suddenly I knew why Uncle Rory had used such fancy vocabulary to tell me to keep quiet: *we were being spied upon.*

I nodded my understanding, and both Gerome David and Uncle Rory nodded back. Uncle Rory kept writing and Gerome David resumed rinsing out his rags, squeezing the water from them as best he could, and then cutting them into bandages, though the work seemed very taxing.

"Twin solar exhibitions pending the onset of precipice-adjacent residence," Uncle Rory whispered.

I hesitated, thinking this through; Uncle Rory had stressed the importance of vocabulary to all Wrecker children; now he was speaking plain English in words that few pirates could discern. I smiled and nodded my understanding; *we were two days from Gibbet Bay.*

"Affirmation offered," I said, nodding to him.

Uncle Rory and Gerome David both smiled.

"Converse summating the nocturnal pinnacle," Uncle Rory said, looking directly at me.

I nodded and turned to leave. Gerome David sniggered as I reached the door. I hesitated and looked back at Gerome David, grinning widely.

"Concurrent visage manifestation amplifies your previous appearance excelling your customary hideous impression," I said wickedly.

Gerome David looked surprised, then smiled widely.

"Verbiage surpassing your universal ignorance falsely reports your stumpy cerebral responsiveness," Gerome David retorted.

Uncle Rory snapped his fingers loudly and pointed toward the door. I took his meaning, but even he was smiling.

That night, at the top spar of the main mast, I clung to the polished wood, one hand on a line, as a dark shape climbed up to join me just below the fluttering pendant. I glanced at the mizzen mast; from his watchful perch, Tom-john's face shined in the starlight, and a brief wave of his hand told me that he knew and approved of my visitor.

Uncle Rory scaled the rigging with mastery, not with the expertise of Tom-john, but with calm certitude. As he joined me on the top spar, he glanced below.

"I don't think that I was seen," Uncle Rory whispered.

"Tom-john saw you," I said, pointing across at him. "Nothing happens in the sheets that he doesn't know of."

"My lightning patient," Uncle Rory said, looking down at Tom-john. "Only fools stay up here in stormy weather."

"He believes that God favors him," I assured Uncle Rory. "He's Captain Angel's most-loyal man; he won't give us away."

"Jeremy Albert, you've got to be careful," Uncle Rory warned, scowling. "Even Angela's men may have hidden motives. We've got to stay silent and not trust anyone ..."

"But they're my friends, our allies ...!"

"Every trust is a risk of betrayal," Uncle Rory said. "We can't risk our lives ... and our family. Stay silent. Keep to yourself. In two days we'll be home, and hopefully, alive, even after the waylay."

"You really think that they'll waylay a man-'o-war?" I asked.

"That's our biggest risk," Uncle Rory said. "If they saw this deck and rigging crowded with sailors, as this ship should be, Grandpa Jack wouldn't dare start the waylay, not even with Hammer and Fist. But there aren't enough pirates aboard to cover the deck, not even with the new recruits from Captain Godsworth. I've been offering obtrusive speculations and then letting my patients blather; I've learned much in just the last day, more than Captain Angel ever revealed. Beware of Captain Angel; she's smarter than she seems, secretive and subtle. She discerns more than just words."

"You know what she wants me to do?"

Uncle Rory smiled grimly.

"I suggested it, not quite openly, but I'm sure that she knows that," Uncle Rory said. "Don't fail; killing Captain Beckett is key to our plan."

"Why?" I asked. "If we're hoping to kill all of Captain Beckett's men in the waylay ..."

"Our only chance depends on confusion," Uncle Rory explained. "While our family rains death from above, we'll be in their sights. If Captain Beckett lives, even in the heat of the waylay, he'll order his men to kill us. Wreckers target first anyone firing up at them; we need the pirates targeting all of their weapons at the cliffs. That'll give us time to swim to the Cave of Riches; we know that it's a deathtrap, but we may not be the only ones to make it inside. Don't reveal us; Grandpa Jack would call off the attack, but that would leave the family vulnerable. We can't signal our presence until all of the pirates are dead."

"What about Angela and Tom-john?"

Uncle Rory stared at me with a grim frown, then slowly gripped my shoulder with unexpected ferocity, anger trembling his voice.

"We ... Angela and I ... have their rescue planned, and it's none of your business; you'll just ruin everything

... again. You have only one chore: kill Captain Beckett right before the waylay, with one shot, and then get inside the cave as fast as you can. The crew's tense; every side is expecting trouble. If you fail, then our whole clan, and our friends, die."

The sun rose bright and clear the next day, and our keel cut a fast track across the sea. Gulls flew overhead, squawking and diving for storm-tossed flotsam littering the waves. Winds billowed our sails, pushing us toward Gibbet Bay. As I stared up at the clear blue sky, my stomach rumbled. I glanced down; Tom-john's bucket was nearly empty, and looked and smelled terrible.

"Tom-john!" I shouted, lifting up his bucket. "I'm going to refill."

"Outside or in?" Tom-john asked from the main spar.

"In, this time," I said. "Our bucket needs washing."

Tom-john laughed, which I took for approval, and I descended down to the deck, carrying the reeking bucket.

The deck was crowded; the weather was perfect, too fine for huddling below decks. All the pirates looked busy; they knew better than to be seen doing nothing, except Zewdnesh, who stood tall and silent by the rail, sniffing the air. Zewdnesh had a far-off look in his eye; he wet a finger with his own spit and held it up into the wind, watching it intently.

"Good weather?" I asked Zewdnesh.

Zewdnesh shook his head.

"One storm has passed, but it was only the feint," Zewdnesh said slowly. "The sea looks calm, but beneath it boils and churns. A great swell approaches; few ships will survive."

"Believe what Zewdnesh says," Tenny said, who was plaiting ropes with Slim and Capsize. "In eleven years, I've never seen him wrong."

I glanced at the perfect weather and found Zewdnesh's prediction doubtful, but I kept my disbelief unspoken. Slicer walked quickly past, glaring at me, and I jumped out of his way, giving him plenty of path. Slicer, however, veered suddenly and bodily walked into Tenny, who was only half of his height. Forcefully bumped, Tenny fell backwards onto his butt, crying out.

"Hey!" Slim and Capsize complained.

Slicer spun and stared as if daring them to challenge him. A dozen other pirates of Captain Beckett's crew appeared suddenly, closing around us from all sides. Angrily Tenny jumped up cursing; I grabbed his arm, trying to restrain him: clearly, this had all been planned.

"No!" I said desperately. "He's sorry ...!"

"Sorry?" Slicer laughed deeply, his grating voice dripping with sarcasm. "Aye, a sorry, one-handed, half-powder load; I've wielded swords bigger than him."

"I'll cut your ...!" Tenny shouted, pulling free, but Slim and Capsize seized Tenny before he fully escaped my grasp.

More pirates gathered, mostly Captain Beckett's men, but also a few of the recruits from Captain Godsworth's crew. Salty, Aiden, and Breakwater had been aft, huddled together, talking in whispers; all three ran forward.

"Hold your tongue, if you hope to need it again," Slicer said to Tenny. "Your life's shorter than your head; once Captain Beckett gets the treasure, then we can clean this ship of disloyal filth."

"That's big talk coming from a kin-slayer," Slim scowled at Slicer. "Filth? You murdered your own grandfather!"

"I'll gut you myself," Slicer snarled, staring at Slim, and he drew a short cutlass.

"You won't," Salty said, and from his belt Salty drew a pistol and pointed it at Slicer.

"What's going on here?" Mr. Roberts shouted, storming down from the helm. "Brawling's forbidden; the lash holds the last word."

"Slicer started it!" Slim shouted, helping hold back Tenny.

"I had to draw my cutlass," Slicer said, pointing at Salty. "Salty aimed a pistol at me."

Every mouth started shouting, a flurry of curses, denials, and threats so loud and multifarious that no one could discern any words. Mr. Roberts shouted the loudest of all, but even his voice was drowned out. Everyone seemed to be arguing, but no one was listening.

A muzzle-blast startled all of us. The pirates drew back and parted, making way. Captain Beckett and Angela stood at the end of the aisle, glaring at everyone; Captain Beckett held a smoking pistol in one hand.

"Fighting amongst my crew?" Captain Beckett shouted, anger deepening his tone.

"Tenny started it, and Angela's men backed him," Mr. Roberts reported. "Salty drew a pistol on Slicer."

Again voices erupted, but Captain Beckett drew another pistol and pointed it at each pirate, even at his own men, until everyone fell silent. The whole crew quieted instantly; none doubted that Captain Beckett would kill.

"You were saying, Mr. Roberts?" Captain Beckett asked.

"Tenny and Salty," Mr. Roberts accused.

"That's not true!" I shouted, and Captain Beckett aimed his pistol at my head.

"Someone give you permission to talk, Tadpole?" Captain Beckett demanded.

I glared but said nothing.

"Master at arms," Captain Beckett said to Angela, "perform your duty."

"Captain, Tenny and Salty weren't fighting each other," Angela said. "This can't have been just my crew."

Captain Beckett aimed his pistol at Angela, but she faced him without flinching.

"You're right," Captain Beckett said slowly to Angela, displaying a false smile. "One of my men should be punished." Captain Beckett glanced back at me, never lowering his pistol, which was aimed at Angela's heart. "Ten lashes each for Tenny and Salty, and five for my precious Tadpole; he needs to learn his place ... and to hold his tongue ... in my crew."

Muted sinister chuckles rose from Captain Beckett's pirates. My heart sank, and I glanced up to see Tom-john watching from above, his pudgy face slack and frowning. Angela stared at the pistol pointed at her chest, heaving harsh breaths in her struggle to restrain her anger. Finally she closed her eyes, squinting as if forcing down a vile medicine, and she angrily pulled her cat from her belt.

"No!" Slim said, but Capsize seized and lifted him, one hand covering Slim's mouth before he could say more.

"Stay!" Salty ordered Slicer as he stepped forward, touching his pistol against Slicer's face.

"Mutiny!" Slicer shouted, but Salty never hesitated.

"No mutiny," Salty said. "I'll take my lashes, but I won't let filth like you touch me."

Salty stepped forward, his pistol aimed to kill, but he only forced Slicer and Captain Beckett's pirates back. After they retreated a few steps, Salty approached the nearest cannon and willingly bent over it, his eyes on Tenny. Tenny glared, sputtering mumbled curses, but he stopped threatening to attack Slicer.

Angela came forward.

"Tie him."

Aidan stepped forward, picked up the end of a rope, and quickly bound Salty's wrists beneath the cannon with tight, single loops.

"I'm sorry," Aidan whispered to Salty.

"Don't make it worse," Salty whispered back to Aidan.

Angela raised her cat; its nine long, braided leather thongs whipped menacingly. I started forward: *if she knew ...! If she'd seen ...!* But Zewdnesh seized my arm and held me back.

"Some winds no sail survives," Zewdnesh said to me.

As I watched helplessly, Salty's aged back was bared. Angela slashed down; all nine strands slapped his back with ripping synchronization. Salty flinched hard, gritting his teeth, but he never once screamed. Nine more bloody lashes followed, each worse than the others, tearing at flesh already torn apart. I flinched almost as badly as Salty. Captain Beckett stood observing each torturous lash, his wide, black-bearded jaw set, his pistol still ready in his hand. When Salty's punishments were complete, Aidan unbound his wrists and Salty stood, shaken and weak, but refusing aid. He walked without a word right through the crowd of Captain Beckett's pirates toward Uncle Rory's cabin, and even Slicer stepped aside for him.

Tenny seemed far more reluctant than Salty, but he resisted very little as Slim and Capsize drug him forward and laid him atop the cannon. I shivered, fearing what would come next. Once bound, Tenny received the same ten lashes that Salty had endured, though he began to cry out after his sixth lash, and ended up blubbering as Slim untied him. Capsize picked up little Tenny and carried him in the same direction that Salty had vanished in.

Everyone turned to look at me, Angela, her face twisted with rage, Captain Beckett with a curious, calm stare, and his pirates watched excitedly, wickedly smiling. Zewdnesh's grip on my arm was a steel shackle, and Breakwater placed a reassuring hand on my shoulder. Aidan and Slim stared at me hopelessly as they approached.

"No!" Uncle Rory's voice shouted, and suddenly he pushed through the crowd of pirates, followed by Gerome David.

"Don't you have patients waiting, doctor?" Captain Beckett challenged.

"They'll keep," Uncle Rory said.

"You're just in time to watch the final punishment," Captain Beckett said, nodding to me.

"Let me talk to him," Uncle Rory said to Captain Beckett. "Please, or he'll only make things worse."

Captain Beckett considered silently, then nodded. Uncle Rory came toward me, but not one of Angela's men released their grips on my arms. Uncle Rory leaned close and whispered right into my ear.

"Say nothing!" Uncle Rory hissed. "Refusing punishment means death; the pain of first-lashes always seems worse than they really are. Scream, cry, anything ... but don't speak, not a word. I'll tend you afterwards. Come."

Uncle Rory glanced at Angela's men and they started pulling me forward. I wanted to appear brave, but I scraped my heels on the deck with all of my strength. Unhindered, they forced me irresistibly toward the deadly cannon, within Angela's cruel reach. Her eyes met mine, and I started to tremble, shaking uncontrollably. I struggled fiercely, but each pirate was stronger than I; my pitiful resistance didn't seem to bother them at all. Uncle Rory helped them hold my hands in place while Aidan bound me to the cannon, now wet with Salty and Tenny's blood.

"Grit your teeth."

"Sorry, mate."

"It won't last long."

I had no idea which of Angela's pirates whispered to me, struggling uselessly as they pulled my shirttail out and up over my shoulders.

"No!" I shouted. "Angela ...!"

A hand cupped tight over my mouth; Uncle Rory held my head before and behind.

"No talking," Uncle Rory said, and then he nodded to Angela.

Fire worse than God's thumps exploded upon my back. I screamed with the first lash and with all four lashes that followed it. I flailed about, banging my chest, arms, and legs against the unyielding iron cannon, but nothing escaped the agonizing lashes that consumed my world and me. Uncle Rory's hands stayed tight about my head, struggling to keep me from cracking my skull against the hard cannon as I flailed, shrieking and bawling, until I lay collapsed upon the gunner's daughter. Barely I was aware when my hands were freed or when I was lifted and carried away.

The next thing that I knew I was blubbering like a child on a bed inside of a cabin, and stabbing fingers were rubbing a stinging greasy ointment into my cuts. My back felt as if I'd been ripped apart, clawed by some monstrous beast. Glimpses of Salty, Tenny, and Gerome David, his eyes as wide as saucers, barely penetrated my consciousness. Despite the pain, I barely flinched; never had I guessed the extremity of exhaustion that I felt; I couldn't move or speak.

"How is he?" Angela's voice floated through my Hell. Salty said something back to her but it was blurred by waves of fire. "Make him understand," Angela finished.

When I was able to glance about, Angela was gone.

"He'll sleep in here tonight," Uncle Rory said to Salty and Tenny. "He'll be fine tomorrow, if a little wiser."

My tears washed the world away.

12

FATE OF THE SEAHAWK

As dawn brightened the sky, Gerome David stood weakly below, upon the deck beside Uncle Rory, as we spied the familiar cliffs of home. I looked upon the cliffs from safely up in the sheets, my back still stinging fiercely. We sailed into the wide inlet; from all of my sharking I recognized our location. The mouth of Gibbet Bay yawned only a few miles inside the inlet, its wide fissure hidden amid the starboard cliffs, the doorstep to the Cave of Riches. I smiled, wondering which of my young cousins was stationed on lookout, and when they'd seen us.

"Mighty cliffs," Tom-john grinned, staring about. "How close to God they rise!"

I forced a grin; many trees near our home had been thumped by God, some thumped into blackened stumps. But the thumping about to hit The Seahawk wasn't God; Wreckers were about to waylay. Tom-john nodded, then stared past me; I followed his gaze. Upon the foredeck stood my target, Captain Beckett, resplendent in his fine purple coat, his wide hat shading his eyes as he scanned the cliffs. Mr. Roberts stood beside him, calling out coordinates on the ship's compass, our deadly Lure clutched in his hand. All of our crew crowded the deck, some in the lower shrouds: Captain Beckett's men, those sailors that we'd acquired from Captain Godsworth's ship, and, standing apart, Captain Angel's men. Tenny, Breakwater, and Capsize looked nervous; I doubted if Uncle Rory had even told them that the Cave of Riches was empty. All that they knew was that if Captain Beckett found a buried treasure chest then he'd kill them all, and they'd die even faster if Captain Angel couldn't assume command after the mutiny.

The Golden Twinkle, their belief that treasure was nearby, sparkled in every pirate's eye. Yet as we sailed closer, worry tingled up my back. Thirty-seven cannons aimed down into Gibbet Bay; even now, Father, Grandpa Jack, and Grandpa Barnaby must be pulling off their rain tarps, unsealing the wooden cups that protected their primers, and giving each gun a final ram. Mother, Great Aunt Pearl, and Olivia Francis were probably snatching up their swags, Margaret-Blythe already reached her point, perhaps taking my usual spot behind the musket-scarred log. Grandma Agnes had already rushed the kids inside our house to hide with

Grandma Lydia until it was all over. Hunter Jack wouldn't be with them; with Gerome David and I missing, he'd probably been given his first set of rifles, preloaded and ready. Kenneth Joel was undoubtedly whispering orders to bring about his imaginary man-'o-war, his cannons already primed and awaiting their target. Cousin Sidney, our powder-master, was eagerly shushing everyone from his place beside the Silver Sprinkle, ordering all of the kids to stay hidden behind their thick, dried brush. Regina Anne was probably in Gerome David's lookout; she had the best eyes of all the adults. Great Aunt Pearl would have her rifles loaded beside an opened keg of powder and basket of shot, seeing The Seahawk as only another vessel possibly carrying her precious oyster-bred treasures. Elviena Joan was probably in Margaret Blythe's usual spot, excited as ever.

Thinking of them, my heart swelled. What if one of them got shot? What if they shot me? Shooting Captain Beckett from much closer range, I'd be in their sights, an unrecognized figure shrouded by smoke and tumult, and my first muzzle-flash would make me their target of choice. But I had to do as Uncle Rory insisted; kill Beckett, then jump overboard and swim for the Cave of Riches. No Wrecker bothered anyone swimming for that deathtrap; when they ran up the Trap, the false stairway, then they'd be better targets; until then, the smoke hid them too well to aim at, and they weren't threatening anyone by escaping into the Cave of Riches.

"There it is: the gap, just like on the map!" Mr. Roberts shouted.

The pirates cheered, all except Angela's men. Angela herself gave a hearty whoop, but her eyes narrowed and she snuck a quick upwards glance at Tom-john and I. I nodded, but she turned away before she could see it. I understood; all of our hopes rested on me now.

"Stations," Tom-john whispered, and he patted my shoulder reaffirmingly. "I've left you a present under your coat; Angela will captain The Seahawk."

Tom-john stood on a spar, grabbed a rope, and swung to the main mast. There he scaled to the very top, unbuttoned his coat, and I spied six pistol-grips sticking out of the top of his belt. *What was he thinking?* We only needed one shot. I had my pistol in the pocket of my coat, but when I lifted my leather garment aside, I stared amazed: under my coat, on the deck of the crowfoot, lay five loaded and primed pistols, a dry powder horn, and pouch of shot.

I glanced up at Tom-john, who nodded to me as we sailed before the open mouth of Gibbet Bay. A hush fell over the crew as they spied Gibbet Bay's inner cliff-walls; the many rattling skeletons hanging from ancient nooses startled them, and they stared horror-stricken. I grinned; well I knew each of those wind-blown racks of bones. Gerome David and Margaret Blythe had named each one when we were kids, and more than once we'd gotten in trouble for repelling down the cliff and playing with them. But their purpose served: all of the pirates were watching the weathered, hanging skeletons, not looking up at the Wrecker rifles and cannons hidden behind the thick camouflage ringing the cliff-tops.

"Drop the sails," Captain Beckett ordered, and pirates jumped to the shrouds and masts, eager to comply. I stayed unmoving, save to cover over my guns. Why had Tom-john given me so many? What plan did he know that I didn't?

I concealed my doubts as Captain Beckett's pirates hurriedly climbed past me. Quickly they furled all our sheets; our momentum was sufficient to enter Gibbet Bay, and any more speed would crash us into the cliff wall under the Silver Sprinkle. The Seahawk slowed to a drift, which the strong current would swirl clockwise around the inside of Gibbet Bay.

My eyes fell upon Angela's men and my confusion grew. Not one of them had jumped to the heights, helping to raise the sails. All stood crowded together, slowly moving backwards toward the poop deck. Salty and Aidan reached the short stairs and ascended, holding closed thick jackets that I'd never seen them wear before. *Why were they going there?* When the waylay struck, they'd want to be near the fore rail, beside Uncle Rory and Gerome David, ready to dive in and swim. The poop was the last place that they'd want to be.

"There!" Mr. Roberts cried. "A waterfall, just like it shows in the map!"

The pirates cheered.

Our sheets furled, we drifted into Gibbet Bay.

Confused, but determined not to fail again, I reached into the pocket of my coat and pulled out my pistol; I'd killed dozens of pirates, and murdering Captain Beckett would avenge our savage capture and the torment of my lashes. My fingers closed on its smooth wooden grip; with this gun I'd redeem myself to Uncle Rory. I didn't pull the trigger yet; I stared down at Captain Beckett, judging my aim, timing the ship's sway, estimating the change in wind-speed as we slid between the tall cliffs. I had to judge everything perfectly; I couldn't afford to miss.

Uncle Rory slowly turned his head and glanced up at me, his expression torn between anxiety and terror. He nodded. I nodded back to him, pulled out my pistol, and aimed it right at the center of Captain Beckett's hat. I had to aim and fire quickly; Captain Beckett's pirates surrounded me, top and bottom, some still hurrying down the lines to the deck.

Uncle Rory smiled in triumph.

A horrible thought startled me. Realization dropped my jaw, making me freeze: I couldn't pull the trigger! *Uncle Rory had lied!* My gunshot wasn't the signal to flee; my murder of Captain Beckett was the trigger to start a mutiny, Captain Angel's men against Captain Beckett's; all of the pirates shooting each other while Wrecker death rained upon them from above. That's why Uncle Rory had ordered me not to talk to any of them, not even to Tom-john! That's why Tom-john had given me so many pistols when I only needed one, and why his belt was stuffed with weapons! Angela's men were taking places along the poop, from where they could shoot half of Captain Beckett's men from relative cover. I was to kill Captain Beckett to start the chaos, and then I was to jump overboard with Uncle Rory and Gerome David. While the three of us swam to safety, Angela's men would slaughter Captain Beckett's pirates, only to make themselves the primary targets of the deadly Wreckers. *If I fired, then all of my friends would die!*

But what could I do? Stop the waylay? If I warned Captain Beckett, then he'd unleash his men upon my family atop the cliffs; their deaths would be my fault. *I was doomed no matter what I chose: kill my family or kill my friends!*

Angela glanced upwards. Her angry gaze fell upon me, in the crowfoot, my exposed pistol aimed at Captain Beckett's head. I didn't fire. Angela's eyes darkened and she reached for her pistol; she was going to kill me.

"*No!*" I cried as loudly as I could, and I threw down my pistol. I jumped for a line, swung myself down, and landed balanced on the main line as only Tom-john could, then rapidly tightrope-walked across the thin line to the main mast. I scaled it quickly as we sailed fully into Gibbet Bay ... into the sights of the Wrecker guns. "*Tom-john, don't shoot! It's a trap! Go overboard! Swim for the cave!*"

Tom-john's expression paled and his eyes flared, startled beyond even God's mighty thumps. I didn't wait to explain further; I grabbed a rope from the mizzen mast and, as Tom-john often had, looped off ten yards, then gripped it as tightly as I could and jumped free. A brief moment I flew aft, and then I dropped, a frightened eternity of falling. The rope jerked, sliced and burned eternal scars into my hands; I cried out, but held firm, although fires of agony shot up my wounded back. The tautened rope swung me aft, and I landed just below the poop, staring up with pain-teared eyes at my armed friends.

"*Don't shoot!*" I shouted at Angela's men. "*Swim for the cave behind the waterfall; it's your only hope!*"

Then I ran fore, the hanging rope still in my burned hands. I'd dropped my pistol, but that didn't matter; my rope-burned hands were wrecked: I couldn't shoot anything.

"Tadpole!" Captain Beckett shouted. "What ...?"

The sudden whack of Grandpa Jack's wooden mallet, followed by the rolling-crunch of the ramp warned me. I ran as fast as I could, half of the crew was staring at me, the other half looking about to detect the source of the strange grinding noise. Angela and Uncle Rory had pistols drawn, both unsurprisingly pointed at me; they'd both said that they'd kill me if I betrayed them.

"*It's a trap!*" I screamed over the last crunch so that every pirate could hear. "*Into the water! Swim for the cave!*"

Hammer smashed aside the dried camouflage as it burst out, free and terrible, directly over The Seahawk. The helmsman had masterfully steered The Seahawk under the starboard cliff, planning to gently turn us around inside narrow Gibbet Bay. Hammer flew out over the edge right over the fore of the ship, a white pillar of solid marble, four feet wide and three feet in diameter, fifty feet above us. Hammer dropped instantly as each pirate cried out in dismay. Everyone, even Angela, jumped away from it. Uncle Rory turned his pistol to face Mr. Roberts, fired, and didn't wait to watch him fall. Uncle Rory lifted Gerome David, and both of them dropped over the side into the familiar waters of home.

I didn't run away; I charged straight at Captain Beckett as Hammer's deadly shadow covered him. Still gripping my rope, I jumped high, swinging fast and hard. Bodily I slammed into Captain Beckett, kicking with both of my feet as hard as I could. I was no match for Captain Beckett's gigantic bulk; our impact knocked me far backwards. His momentum was barely faltered, but it was enough: Hammer fell straight down upon him. Captain Beckett cried out, a deep, terror-filled shout, before the great segment of ancient Roman pillar struck, smashing atop him, crashing through the upper deck, the lower decks, and out through the hull. Hammer's crushing impact tossed The Seahawk like a toy, tipping it forward as it punched through, splashing a great spray of seawater up through its splintery holes.

"*No!*" Angela cried, seeing the destruction, and then the first cannon blasted. A ball smashed into the deck, piercing a hole as shattered timbers blasted into an unlucky pirate. He cried out and fell, and then a second cannon blasted, and an eruption of gunfire followed.

"*Traitor!*" Angela cried, pointing her gun at me.

"*Uncle Rory betrayed you!*" I shouted at her. "*Swim for the cave, if you want to live!*"

Doubt clouded her features, but only for a second. Angela jumped to the rail and, a pistol in each hand, she instantly dove overboard, a flash of beauty that splashed deep into Gibbet Bay. A loud scrape ripped against the hull; our helmsman had been shot, and gunfire suddenly rained upon us, and The Seahawk, the great man-'o-war, tossed by Hammer, rebounded against the cliff to the far side of Gibbet Bay. Angela's men were still on the poop, but all of the noise in the world couldn't drown all thirty-seven Wrecker cannons nor the explosions as the iron balls blasted decks and masts apart. A fierce sting stabbed my arm like a dull knife; I'd been shot, but I couldn't let wounds stop me. I cursed, waved at Angela's men to follow me, and then I heeded them no longer. A thunderous blast struck near me, firing a shower of wooden slivers as I headed for the port rail.

The main mast had been hit, and snapped lines tore free of the rigging; the whole mast toppled. Tom-john

shouted amid the thunderous chorus as he fell, riding
the mast down, wildly waving a feather in one hand and a
pistol in the other. Madly I jumped over the rail,
flipping as I fell, curling into a ball so that I didn't break
my neck when I hit. I splashed into the wet; water,
foam, and bubbles muted the explosions above, salt
burning into my many wounds: arm, back, and injured
pride. Then the main mast struck the bay; our long,
bright pennant splashed colorfully before me. I ignored
it and swam deep; I'd done all that I could.

I wasn't the only one swimming; Slim swam on my
left, a sailor from Captain Godsworth's crew on my right.
We reached the lower steps and I pushed both of them
aside to dash up the familiar steps into the safety of the
Cave of Riches behind the Silver Sprinkle. As I ran
inside, Captain Angel grabbed my wounded arm and
threw me against the cave's wall.

"*The Seahawk's my ship!*" Angela screamed.

"The Seahawk's dead," I replied.

Another crunching-rumble echoed; all thirty-seven
cannons had finished firing, only the crack of musket
and pistol-fire blasted. We both looked out through the
spilling Silver Sprinkle, seeing half of the pirates still
aboard the wounded man-'o-war vainly shooting up at
the protected Wrecker summits. The Seahawk had
drifted against the port cliff, and suddenly Hammer's
twin, Fist, smashed out, hanging only a moment in
midair before it plummeted. Fist's crashing punch rang
the death-knell of the powerful ship; the hull of The

Seahawk split, its timbers shattering. The mighty man-'o-war tilted wildly, waters rushing inside, and began to sink. More pirates, of all three crews, rushed past us as they charged inside our cave, not pausing to stare as Angela stood with her fingers around my throat, a knife drawn from her boot-top, ready to kill me. Behind her, I glimpsed Uncle Rory, who glared at me as if he'd gladly murder me ... if Angela didn't.

Suddenly The Seahawk exploded, engulfed in a great flash of timber-flinging smoke and fire. Uncle Rory had fused the powder-room; The Seahawk was dead. Black smoke filled Gibbet Bay.

"It's not over!" I shouted at Angela, and I pulled free of her, jumped to the mouth of the cave and shouted so loudly that I thought my lungs would burst:

"*Parley!*"

A musketball ricocheted off the wall into my leg, knocking me over, burning into my flesh; *Margaret Blythe!* I silently cursed.

"Parley!" I shouted again. *"Parley!"*

Grandpa Barnaby's shouts echoed out over Gibbet Bay. All firing stopped; every man-jack still aboard The Seahawk lay dead on its ruined, burning timbers.

"Muskets down! Respect parley!" Grandpa Barnaby shouted. "You ... in the cave; what do you want?"

"*Silence!*" I shouted back. "*My name is Jeremy Albert Wrecker, and I want silence!*"

No sound met this declaration. I glanced back; Angela, Uncle Rory, Gerome David, Slim, Tenny,

Capsize, Zewdnesh, Aidan, and more than a dozen other pirates stood glaring at me, shocked, murder in their eyes. I swallowed hard. More than half of us were neither family nor Angela's men; if I dared reveal the truth then they'd kill us for certain, starting with me.

"We're not dead yet," I said to them all, and I staggered to my feet, clinging to the wall of the cave-mouth, fighting to ignore the painful wounds of musketballs in my right arm and left calf. I pushed off toward them and they moved aside. I struggled to the back of the Cave of Riches, dug through the loose dirt that I'd often played in, and then returned. In my hand, I held Grandma Agnes' hangover-proof grog, the rum spiced with cinnamon and pepper to hide its taste of deadly belladonna berries. "I can get us out of this."

"*You got us into this!*" Slicer shouted, and he pointed a long, naked cutlass at me. "You .. and them ...!" he pointed to Uncle Rory and Gerome David. "And Angela! You're all in this together!"

I handed him the bottle of poisoned rum. If he and the other pirates would just take one drink each, then soon they'd be dying, and we'd be free.

Slicer took the bottle and lifted it up, looking suspiciously at it.

"How did you know this was back there?" Slicer demanded.

Suddenly Slicer threw the bottle hard against the cave wall; it shattered against the stone, spraying poisoned rum and broken glass. Slicer drew back his sword, ready to run me through.

"Do you think that this is what we wanted?" I shouted, trying to confuse him, the only hope that I had left. "Angela wanted to captain The Seahawk, not sink her! *This is Beckett's fault!*"

This pronouncement startled Slicer and the other glaring pirates.

"Captain Beckett knew this?" Angela suddenly spoke up. I stared at her; only talk could delay Slicer's revenge.

"That's right," I said.

"Why would Captain Beckett sink his own ship?" Pete demanded, backing up Slicer with a curved dagger.

"Beckett tried to betray the Wreckers," I said. "That's my family, up there on the cliffs. They've got four caves stuffed with treasure. Captain Beckett recognized the map the first time he saw it; he knew my Grandpa Barnaby; they sailed together for years. He led you here as a ploy, intending to reunite with Grandpa Barnaby, then betray him and kill my whole family."

"Why follow the map, then?" Slicer sneered.

"Grandpa Barnaby never told him where we lived," I said. "I saw him give Grandpa Barnaby the secret signal as we sailed into the bay, but everyone knows how treacherous Captain Beckett was. Grandpa Barnaby knew; Beckett always betrayed his friends. But Grandpa Barnaby didn't know that we were aboard The Seahawk, or he wouldn't have attacked."

"*Yer a liar!*" Slicer growled threateningly.

"Who cares if he's lying?" Aidan asked. "We've got nothing but a few wet guns, no powder, and no ship!"

"You have me," I said. "Let me talk to them. My family's been waylaying ships here for a hundred years; you can ransom us for all of the treasure that you can carry; we've got plenty."

Amid their glares at me, the pirates glanced sideways at each other. Slicer snarled savagely.

"I'll go first," I said to Slicer. "We'll go up the stairs, you right behind me with your sword, and you can talk to them yourself."

"Don't," Pete said, fingering his curved dagger. "Let's kill them now!"

Several pirates cheered Pete's suggestion.

"And then what?" Uncle Rory asked. "We're your only hope; kill us ... and how will you escape?"

The pirates glared, weapons barely restrained, anger unrequited.

"Let me try," I said. "What have you got to lose?"

"We need hostages," Aidan said.

"*Yer one of them!*" Slicer shouted at Aidan.

"We're pirates, not Wreckers," Aidan said.

"That's right," Angela said, stepping forward. "We can ..."

"*You're not captain here!*" Slicer shouted at her, pointing his cutlass at Angela. "*Be silent! You've never been good for more than one thing!*"

"I've gotten pirates out of worse scrapes than this," Angela reminded him.

"We can't trust you," Slicer said. "I'm captain now, until we're out of this mess. Tadpole, you go first. Pete, keep a few lads here to watch these traitors. If any of them tries anything, kill 'em. Tadpole, you're with me."

I nodded; anything was better than dying. I stared hesitantly at the point of his cutlass, expecting Slicer to stab me through, but he held it aside for me to pass. Angela stared at me, her face resolute, but fear finally shadowed her dark eyes. Uncle Rory and Gerome David glared, each angrier than the other, but both impotently stood aside as I passed by them. If this didn't work, and we survived, then everyone would kill me. Unfortunately, Grandma Agnes' hangover-proof grog had been my last hope; I had no idea what to do.

I gritted my teeth against the burn of the musketball in my leg as I limped to the mouth of the Cave of Riches.

"Father!" I cried from the mouth of the cave. "Mother! Grandpa Jack! Grandpa Barnaby!"

"Keel-haul them!" Kenneth Joel shouted, but a curt growl from Grandpa Barnaby silenced him. I glanced at Slicer; Kenneth Joel's shout hadn't amused him.

"It's me, Jeremy Albert! Don't shoot; I'm coming out!"

I stepped out onto the shelf behind the Silver Sprinkle and waved up at them. Faces that I'd feared I'd never see again rose and waved back at me.

"We want treasure, weapons, powder, and horses!" Slicer shouted.

"Don't shoot!" I shouted to everyone, especially at Margaret Blythe. "They have Uncle Rory and Gerome David! We've agreed to parley."

"What terms of parley?" Grandpa Barnaby shouted.

"We're coming up the stairs," I shouted. "Don't shoot; I've a cutlass at my back."

"*Nobody shoot!*" Grandpa Barnaby shouted to the family.

I nodded to Slicer and then I climbed up the worn, chiseled stairs. Slicer came out right behind me, Pistol, Chuckie, Bard, and Hardback right behind him. I glanced out at the burning wreck of The Seahawk, the man-'o-war's smoking aft was caught on the rocky port cliff, its bow already underwater. All three masts had fallen, one collapsed toward us, the other two toppled toward the mouth of Gibbet Bay. The shattered deck lay littered with the corpses of pirates that had tried to fight under ambush, not realizing the hopelessness of the trap that had claimed a hundred ships. The choppy waters of Gibbet Bay ran pink and white, frothing as the breakers hit the rocks. Amid the ruin floated one thick, short man in a wide blue leather jacket, face-up, his long arms spread out as if crucified upon the water, five unfired pistols still in his belt; Tom-john, fallen in the waylay. Tears filled my eyes, but I limped up each painful step. Slicer, Pistol, Chuckie, Bard, and Hardback followed close behind me.

I had no idea how I was getting out of this. I ascended, limping worse than I really felt, which was bad enough, but when Slicer and the others reached the Trap, then they'd see that the rest of the stairs upwards were false, a two-inch wide stairway carved into the rock which no one could ascend with the guns of the every Wrecker aimed at their backs. When I reached the top, I'd die, but, once Grandpa Barnaby had killed these leaders, Uncle Rory and Angela could easily outwit Pete and those who'd remained behind.

I silently cursed myself: *I shouldn't have done it.* I should've shot Captain Beckett and saved my family, even if it meant the death of my new friends. I'd been a fool, but I'd never had any friends that I wasn't related to, and most of all, I'd wanted to save Tom-john. Now I'd gotten him killed ... and myself as well.

Slowly we climbed to the Trap. I estimated no more than five of Captain Beckett's men had stayed in the Cave of Riches to watch Uncle Rory, Gerome David, Angela, and her men; they could deal with them. But I'd come to the end of my journey.

"Wha ...! The stairs!" Slicer cried. "It's a trap! What are you pulling, Tadpole?"

"Nothing," I said loudly, clear enough for everyone to hear me. "*Wreckers: don't let these men back into the cave! Shoot me if you have to: don't let them ...!*"

"Hold yer fire!" Slicer shouted, grabbing me and using me as a shield, his cutlass across my throat.

"Anyone shoots and Tadpole gets it first! Back, you dogs! Back to the cave!"

"*Margaret!*" I shouted, straining to keep from being pulled backwards. "*I'm dead anyway! Save Rory and Gerome! Kill me!*"

Suddenly a single explosion blasted: Margaret Blythe shot me in the head. The force knocked me face-first onto the top of the Trap as blood splattered my face and shoulder. Slicer's cutlass slashed across my neck; no bee could match his sting. I fell, certain that I was dead.

Blasts of musket-fire erupted from all around the summit. Every Wrecker fired, and a musketball ricocheted off the top landing inches from my hand. *My family, my friends, or myself: I couldn't save everyone.*

Strangely, I didn't feel dead. The wetness of my own blood streamed down my face, but with little pain. I reached up and probed for the wound, but found only blood-splattered hair. Despite the gunfire, which I no longer feared, I rolled over and looked behind; Slicer lay against the wall, his face torn open by a musketball that had struck right between his eyes. The force of that impact had knocked me nearly senseless, but the blood and bits of flesh streaming from the side of my head was Slicer's, not mine. *Margaret Blythe had saved my life.*

My hand touched my neck; again I'd been wounded, a deep cut on the right side of my neck, but in the muscle, not across my windpipe. It hurt like Hades, but I'd survive.

Slicer's followers fared no better than their leader. Every Wrecker had blown them apart before they made it down one level; all had collapsed on the Trap or the upper stairs, dead or dying.

With an agonized cry, Pete came flying out of the Cave of Riches right through the Silver Sprinkle, clutching his chest with blood-painted hands. Shouts and curses came from within as Pete splashed into Gibbet Bay, and then Gerome David jumped out onto the ledge before the cave.

"We've got them!" Gerome David cried to every Wrecker. "Get down here!"

"Lower the ladder!" Grandpa Jack cried, and figures raced along the top of the cliffs on both sides, hurrying to get down. Father and Cousin Sidney didn't wait, but dove clear off the top of Gibbet Bay into the water. Hunter Jack followed them a moment later, diving headfirst, the point of a long sword leading his plunge.

I didn't care about any of them anymore. Despite my wounds, I lurched up and dropped off the Trap. The salt water flamed inside my wounded back, calf, arm, and neck, and my hands were still barely-usable, burned from the last rope that I'd swung on, dropping from the sails of the mighty Seahawk. But I'd been swimming since I was three, and I was a Wrecker. Underwater, I kicked off against the rock wall and swam hard; I had one friend left, and if I could save him, then I would. Most men don't die instantly to musketballs,

and I prayed as I swam out amid the flotsam and
wreckage.

Tom-john was floating face-up in the water, eyes
closed, looking like many a corpse that I'd sharked. I
seized and shook him, but received no response. I
searched him for bleeding wounds; Tom-john had taken
a musketball low on the ribs which had penetrated deep.
Desperate, I started pulling him back, when suddenly
hands grabbed me. I struggled against them.

"Easy! Let us help!"

Margaret Blythe swam up on one side, Hunter Jack
on the other. They grabbed Tom-john and started to
pull him toward the steps. I ducked under to let them
pass overhead, and then swam after them.

"What do you want with this corpse?" Margaret
Blythe asked.

I didn't answer, saving my breath. If I let them see
how fast my strength was failing then they'd release Tom-
john to rescue me.

"Uncle Rory!" I cried as we reached the lower steps.
The ladder had been lowered; Grandpa Barnaby and
Kenneth Joel ran to help pull us up onto the steps.
"Uncle Rory, it's Tom-john! He's been shot!"

Uncle Rory came, looked over the wound, and
shook his head.

"He's dying, Jeremy," Uncle Rory said.

"You can save him!" I shouted.

"Perhaps, but for what? He's not a Wrecker ..."

"He's my friend!"

After a second's hesitation, Uncle Rory helped lift Tom-john, and everyone but me carried him up to the second landing.

"What about the others?" Angela demanded. "Keeler and Breakwater?"

"I'll look for them," I said, but I staggered, almost falling. Father grabbed me.

"You're hurt," Father said.

"I'll live," I said. "Please; I have to go."

"Take the boat," Father said. "Mother, go with them; everyone carries a musket. Margaret Blythe, you go, too."

"This isn't the Wrecker way," Cousin Sydney warned.

"Waylaying our own kinfolk isn't the Wrecker way, either," Father said, looking at me. "I make decisions when I know the facts; until then, I take orders."

I met Father's eyes and thankfully nodded.

"Grandma Agnes, lower the boat!" Margaret Blythe shouted up to those who remained above.

Behind us, Uncle Rory was describing what had happened as he tended Tom-john, how we'd been shanghaied, and he didn't hide that I'd started it all, or that Gerome David had almost died. I couldn't listen; I looked over at Margaret Blythe, who stood near me, waiting for them to winch down our rowboat.

"I'm sorry," Margaret Blythe said.

"Sorry?" I asked. "My head wasn't two inches from Slicer's face when you fired. That was the best shot that I've ever seen."

"Oh, um... thanks," Margaret Blythe frowned, and she pointed at Tom-john. "I meant ... *I shot your friend ... as the main mast was falling.*"

Despite myself, I grinned; I hated that Tom-john got hurt, but I couldn't blame Margaret Blythe for shooting a pirate. Besides, striking a sailor riding a falling mast; that was a great shot, too. But I wasn't worried; Uncle Rory would save him: *he had to.*

The next hour was extremely uncomfortable, not only because I had to wade among the fallen, looking for the remainder of Angela's men, but because every time that I spotted a wounded pirate that wasn't one of Angela's crew, Mother, Grandma Agnes, or Margaret Blythe shot him dead. I found my friends on the poop deck; Keeler was dead, and, no one, not even Uncle Rory, could hope to save Breakwater with as many holes as he was bleeding from. Breakwater tried to speak, but couldn't. He died before my eyes.

Few pirates were left alive to kill. Of Captain Beckett, Hammer had squashed him flat; I wondered if his hat would still be atop his corpse when we winched Hammer back up the cliff; if so, then I'd keep it for myself. But I was worried about Angela and her men, my first true friends. My loyalty would remain with Grandpa Jack and the Wrecker clan, but I'd always boast of being a crewman of Captain Angel.

The next morning, I awoke in my own bed beside Gerome David and my younger cousins, whose jostling as they climbed out of bed awoke me. I sat up, hearing the familiar clatter of forks and plates.

"Jeremy Albert, you stay in that bed!" Great Aunt Pearl admonished me. "You need to heal."

I blinked my eyes and smiled; I was home at last. Half of the Wrecker elders and all of our children were sitting at our big table, eating and discussing our prisoners. Great Aunt Pearl and Grandma Agnes were still cooking.

"Where's Tom-john ... and Angela?" I asked.

"You've no business with them, fool boy," Great Aunt Pearl said.

I threw back the covers defiantly, determined to find my friends. My wounds burned and stung as I slid off the bed, my neck unable to turn to either side, and my ankle so stiff that it barely held my weight, but no wounds stopped me.

"Get back in bed!" Great Aunt Pearl ordered. "You're not healed!"

I ignored her and tried to hobble past the end of my bed, but Great Aunt Pearl came over and grabbed my arm as if to force me back into bed. I gazed at her sternly, fury in my eyes, and spoke with a voice to make even Angela tremble.

"Take your hands off of me!"

Great Aunt Pearl ignored me and pushed harder, with half the elders and children frozen, watching with open mouths and utensils half-raised. I held my ground, seized Great Aunt Pearl's wrist, and with only slightly-greater pain from my wounds, I pried her aged grip from my arm.

"*I'm going to see my friends,*" I growled fiercely.

Great Aunt Pearl staggered backwards, staring as if seeing me for the first time. I limped to the door, opened it, and then turned back to look at Great Aunt Pearl.

"I'd never hurt you," I said to Great Aunt Pearl, "but I have to do this."

"Jeremy Albert's not a boy anymore," Grandma Lydia said as I walked outside.

A small cabin-bed was set up next to a thick tree by the Silver Sprinkle. Tom-john was in the bed, asleep, and the last of Angela's men sat beside him or leaned against the tree. As I walked up to them, I noticed that heavy iron manacles were fastened around their ankles, tethered by stout chains to the tree. Salty was wearing a bloody sling. Capsize looked like he'd gotten shot twice; wide bandages covered his chest and left arm. Cousin Sidney sat not far from them, a saber and two muskets beside him.

"*Tadpole!*" Slim jumped up and shouted excitedly. "Help us, dear friend ... shipmate! We don't deserve to die!"

"I swam!" Capsize said joyously. "While The Seahawk was sinking, I swam!"

"They won't hurt me," I said to Cousin Sidney, and then I joined them at Tom-john's bedside. "How is he?"

"Bless that Rory, ship's doctor," Aidan said. "He's a miracle-worker; said that Tom-john's gonna be fine. He tended him half of the night and pried the musketball from Salty's arm before he went to bed."

"How is it?" I asked Salty.

"Hurts, but better than being executed," Salty said with a glance at Cousin Sidney.

"Don't worry," I said although, chained by strangers, they had nothing to do but worry. "Where's Angela?"

"Captain Angel be with your Master Jack," Tenny said.

I nodded and went looking. The Seahawk, the great man-'o-war, the only ship that I'd ever sailed upon, lay blown, burned, holed, and sunk in Gibbet Bay. It must've settled in the night; it was fully underwater, save for its floating masts, though it was so big that its wide deck could be clearly seen through the choppy water. Hunter Jack and Margaret Blythe were standing on the lowest step, staring at it; both knew better than to enter the bloody water until after the sharking.

I found Captain Angel walking around the remains of the Roman gardens with Grandpa Jack, Grandpa Barnaby, Father, and Uncle Rory. They all fell silent as I approached, and their dark stares implied full knowledge of my guilt.

"*Why are my shipmates chained?*" I demanded.

Angela smiled widely, a great change from her usual forbidding expression. Father and my grandfathers frowned and Uncle Rory scowled.

"You disobeyed me!" Uncle Rory snarled.

"You were going to kill my friends," I challenged. "They saved Gerome David ... and you."

"*You had my orders!*" Uncle Rory countered. "*We could've all died ... again!*"

"I obey orders," I said. "I'll kill anyone you want, but not my ... *our friends.* Grandpa Jack, if you want me to, I'll leave, just like Grandpa Barnaby, and go out to sea with my friends."

"They can't go," Grandpa Barnaby said flatly. "You know that, Jeremy Albert; they're not Wreckers."

"*Shipmates are family,*" I said icily to Grandpa Barnaby. "*You taught me that.*"

Father snapped his fingers, glaring at me. I fell silent.

"Son, you've grown a lot since you left here, but Wreckers don't disrespect their elders," Father said.

"I don't mean any disrespect, but I can't let you kill my friends. If you try, then you'll have to kill me, too."

They all glanced at each other, exchanging silent understandings. I stared at each of them in turn, finally looking at Angela, and a brilliant idea struck me.

"You can't kill Angela's men," I said. "They're her family."

"But Angela isn't a Wrecker," Father said.

I took a deep breath and faced them, ready for their arguments.

"I'll marry Angela," I announced, raising myself up as tall and proudly as I could. "Then we'll all be related."

To my amazement, they all burst out laughing, long and deeply. As they laughed, Grandpa Jack held out a key to me; the key to their chains.

"Welcome to manhood, Jeremy Albert Wrecker," Grandpa Jack said in his slow, droning voice, and every word startled me. "Here, take the key; we were on our way to free your friends, who are going to be your cousins. But you don't have to marry Angela; she's already engaged."

"B-but ...," I stammered, "how will Angela marrying Tom-john make us cousins?"

"*Tom-john?*" Angela laughed. "Marry Tom-john? You know better than any how mad he is."

Angela's merry peals joined the laughter of the men.

"B-but ... who ...?"

"Me," Uncle Rory said softly, and he took Angela's arm in his, and she gave it full-willing. I gasped and stared in disbelief.

"*You?*" I asked, astounded. "*But ... you plotted to kill her!*"

"I plotted to kill you both, and your brother," Angela said, smiling wickedly.

"*What?*" I exclaimed. "*No! You helped us ...!*"

"I saw through her plan right away," Uncle Rory said, grinning wryly.

"No, you didn't," Angela teased.

"I assumed it," Uncle Rory smiled at her.

"*B-but ... you kissed me!*" I said to Angela.

"Never trust the kisses of a woman who kills," Angela grinned. "You allowed yourself to be deceived because you wanted me; you're a man, but you still have much growing to do."

Angela released Uncle Rory, and then she hugged me tightly. I frowned, feeling very childish in her strong arms.

"Thank you," Angela smiled down at me. "Your proposal was most-flattering, but your uncle and I are a better match, more-worthy of each other. I'll be your aunt ... and you'll be my favorite nephew. Don't worry; I know many young girls that would be thrilled to marry you, and your brother, when you're ready ... pretty girls ... worthy of the Wrecker clan."

"You'll always be my ... Captain Angel," I said, secretly regretting not marrying her.

Angela became a Wrecker three days later, marrying Uncle Rory before our whole family and her pirates, with Salty giving her away. Grandpa Jack officiated, and afterwards we held a great feast. No demolition of The Seahawk continued that day or the day after, although Cousin Sidney had devised elaborate plans to blow its remaining hull into sections. I couldn't help at all; it was weeks before I could easily use my hands again, and a month before I could walk without limping. My arm healed much faster than my calf, and with a cane to help me walk, I took Slim, Tenny, Capsize, Zewdnesh, Aidan, and Salty all around our clifftop, showing them all of my childhood hiding places and all of the excavations that we'd begun, trying to find the four hidden treasure-caves sealed by Grandpa Jack.

With their help, and Angela's, we dismantled The Seahawk as fast as we could've salvaged a fishing boat. It was obvious that their loyalty still fell upon Captain Angel, who quickly took charge and ordered them about as if still aboard ship.

Father and Grandpa Barnaby walked down the main road to the lowlands after The Seahawk was cleared from Gibbet Bay, and twenty days later, before the first snow, they returned with two new horses, a sturdy new cart, and two beautiful young women, both of whom Angela had known from her brothel-days, and the pleasure that my new bride gave me washed away any regrets that I had about not marrying Angela.

Tom-john alone remained unhappy. For months after Angela's wedding, even in the deep snows of winter, Tom-john could be found out on the icy cliffs, climbing snow-laden trees and staring out at the frigid sea longingly, watching every ship sail past, and insisting that we leave him alone. Angela told Tom-john that she'd only married Uncle Rory to spare his life, and that he'd always be her true love, which I doubted, but Tom-john wouldn't be appeased. Tom-john obeyed Angela and never left our cliffs, but his spirit slowly crumbled.

Spring came early, warm and leafy, and Grandpa Jack made a monumental decision. It was time to seed another treasure map at a distant port city, and Cousin Sidney, Father, and Gerome David were selected for the journey. After the mess that I'd caused, I couldn't blame them for not choosing me, but watching my brother leave without me irked.

"We can't afford to take an idiot every time," Gerome David chided me.

"You were only chosen because you're expendable," I chided back.

But Gerome David's departure wasn't what bothered me. By unanimous consent of the elders, and Grandpa Jack's incredible declaration, Tom-john was going to be allowed to depart with the party ... but not come back. After getting to know Tom-john as well as I had, that he was as trustworthy as he was mad, the whole family agreed to break its long-standing rule and allow Tom-john, although he wasn't a Wrecker, to return to the sea.

Great Aunt Pearl presented Tom-john with one of her precious black pearl rings, and Grandpa Jack gave him a small bag of gold, enough to live out several years in luxurious sea-side comfort, but we all knew that he'd waste it on rum and sign aboard the first vessel that sailed. Angela made Tom-john promise to return, if he ever tired of the sea, but that, too, was a false hope.

The morning of their departure, Cousin Sidney, Father, Gerome David, and Tom-john packed food, clothes, and a cartful of scavenged treasures, and prepared to ride down the long trail to the flatlands, pulled by both horses. Gerome David carried a salvaged bible with another false treasure map folded inside it.

"No matter where you go, you'll always carry my heart," Angela said to Tom-john. "Farewell, my beloved Pope Captain Prince Tom-john the Blessed."

"Farewell, my beautiful Captain Angel," Tom-john said, and with a soft kiss, they parted forever.

"Farewell, Tadpole," Tom-john said, and he hugged me long and hard.

"May God thump you every day," I said, clinging to him as long as I could.

That was the last I ever saw of Tom-john, riding away with Cousin Sidney, Father, and Gerome David. They reported that he gave them back most of his gold, keeping only enough to buy passage on a great merchantman sailing toward distant lands. I think of him every day, romping among the rigging, clinging to masts through tempest and hurricane, singing to the seagulls, collecting their tail-feathers for his too-small hat, and calling for God to thump him. I learned from Tom-john that madness and bravery are often the same; when God finally thumps Tom-john for the last time then the bravest man that ever lived will leave this world forever.

For myself, I became a father six times, and I remained a Wrecker, but I never waylaid again. Aidan had been born a farmer, and he, Uncle Rory, and I expanded our fields many times over, and farming became as big a part of our lives as piracy. I taught my kids to shoot and to uphold the Wrecker traditions, but I also told them stories of Chad Mathew, Keeler, and Breakwater to insure that they understood the value of every human life. The Wrecker family grew and thrived, and Captain Angel eventually became our titular head of house, although by then she little-resembled the muscular terror that had wielded the cat-of-nine. Under her, the Wrecker family prospered and grew, forever realizing the words of our great founder, Zachary William Wrecker:

Blessed be God Almighty from whom all swags flow.

THE END.

Jay Palmer

ABOUT THE AUTHOR

Born in Tripler Army Medical Center, Honolulu, Hawaii,
Jay Palmer works as a technical writer in the software
industry in Seattle, Washington. Jay enjoys parties, reading
everything in sight, woodworking, obscure board games,
and riding his Kawasaki Vulcan. Jay is a knight in the
SCA, frequently attends writer conferences, SciFi
Conventions, and he and Karen are both avid ballroom
dancers. But most of all, Jay enjoys writing.

50892904R00150

Made in the USA
San Bernardino, CA
07 July 2017